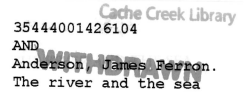

THE RIVER AND THE SEA

James Ferron Anderson

RETHINK PRESS

First Published in Great Britain 2012
by Rethink Press

© Copyright James Ferron Anderson

Cover Photograph by Mark Wragg (istockphoto.com/wragg)

For my dear June, my love, my support.

But his Captain's hand on his shoulder smote:
'Play up! play up! and play the game!'

Vitaï Lampada
SIR HENRY NEWBOLT, 1892

CHAPTER ONE

A JANUARY MORNING. Terrible cold, terrible hunger. The constants. At the back of those constants, another. Her. Sarah. Far away, eight hundred miles to the south. I opened my eyes and there, across the cabin, her husband, Edward, wrapping rags of blanket around his legs, tying them on with twine from our old parcels. Edward, who had hardly been home a month before planning to leave again. Pulling the capote down over himself, picking up the .303. Outside the north wind roared on. At the door he stopped, his hand on the wooden latch, and looked back, his eyes going around the walls, over the table with its mass of sorted bones, on to Harry in his bunk, his face to the wall. He came to me and saw me awake.

'I'm going out,' he said. Quietly, to not waken Harry I suppose. 'You never know.' His tongue moved across the cracked lips. 'One can't just stay here.' I had nothing to say to him, and after a while he turned away again to the door and raised the latch. I waited to hear him say some last, ridiculous, thing. 'Keep resting your foot,' he said. Then, 'It must be hell not to be able to get about.' Everything was hell. Edward, this is a world of frozen hell. The wind snapped the door out of his hand, flung it against the wall, and snow roared in. Edward's head swung back to Harry, as if to check he had not disturbed him. Then he went outside and got his weight to the door, and closed it behind him.

An hour, two hours later, Harry turned his face from the wall. I was still awake, lying there, busy hating him. Hating Edward. Hating everything. Hating myself, for being a fool. I consumed hatred, as it consumed me. I closed my eyes so I wouldn't see Harry. When I opened them again he was at the

1

heap of bones on the table, moving, examining them. He held up some small bone, some pale stick from a fox or a hare or wolverine. He laid it down and his hands moved on with his sorting. There was no food there, sort them as he might. No food, Harry. I hadn't eaten for four days, whatever he had found among the bones. Edward hadn't eaten.

I could hear the crackle of the stove but could feel no heat from it. I dozed on, then sat up, my throat raw. Harry was back in his bunk, eyes closed. The fire was out, but there was a tin can where snow had been melted, and it was still half full and just thinly iced over. I drank all of it.

I should get more snow for the can. Get the fire going again. I should take the other rifle and limp on my bad foot outside and lie in the snow and hope some slow and foolish animal would pass in this flat and barren place. We were on a caribou trail. Harry had said so. I went back to the bunk and got under the red blankets. When I woke next Edward was coming in and calling to Harry that he had seen wolf tracks.

'If there's wolf tracks there's caribou,' said Harry. 'What did I tell you?' He squatted on his bunk, his knife out, hacking at a bone, poking at the marrow in it and eating the tiny scrapings he found. Old entrails were on his blankets, dried blood down his coat. 'What did I tell you? Wouldn't you say so too, Jack? You're an old hand in the North.' He turned back to his cousin. 'Didn't I say, Edward? Before the end of the month. Where? How many? Going in what direction?'

'Four, or maybe five,' said Edward. 'About five or six hundred yards upstream and heading away.'

'We'll get the caribou.' He licked the end of the knife blade. 'And maybe wolf as well. You'd scare them off. Either of you. The old dog will get them.' His gums were dark and sunken. He hadn't worn his false teeth since we had left Waterways. 'Tomorrow. I'll be gone by daylight.'

When I woke in mid-morning he was still there, mending a snowshoe.

'Harry can't go out without being prepared,' said Edward. He had seen me looking. An hour later Harry put a strip of boiled hide in his pocket and put on the snowshoes and took the rifle and went out. I took the crutch and hobbled along the trapline as far as I could go but there was nothing there. Harry came back after dark had fallen and he had no news of either wolf or caribou. The next afternoon while Edward and I were cutting firewood we heard three shots. A half hour later Harry came stumbling towards us. He had been crossing the river ice when he had seen two caribou, killed one and wounded the other.

We all left together, but I fell behind. I found them later upriver with the carcass partly stripped. I butchered with them, blood over our sleeves, splattered on our faces. It was a hard winter for these poor beasts too, and there wasn't much meat. We wrapped up what we had cut, and Edward and I started to pack it back. Harry sat over the animal with the rifle. Wolves would have it if he didn't, he said, and would have it anyway in the night. I was the one who could hardly walk, but I said nothing. We returned and packed the rest back to the cabin. The wind had risen even more, and snow was falling heavily.

I would wear all the clothes I had, cover myself in anything I could find, my empty stomach aching, my cut foot too frozen to mend, and I would think of far-away Footner. Of the warmth of its endless sun, of the dusty brightness of its long days, of its free, un-hungry English residents, wanting nothing more than to grow a few apples and hunt coyotes and pretend they were foxes, and play cricket and idle and make-believe they were still in England. What was so wrong with that? Those innocent people. I would think of my beautiful Sarah. Always Sarah.

How will I describe her, let you see her, in this flicker film of memory? I could say straight-backed, slim, serious looking, then breaking... not photographing as well as she looked in... hair waving... What would be the point? She was Sarah. I'll tell you about the first time I saw her.

THE MORNING OF WEDNESDAY, 24TH APRIL 1918

I kept a little journal then, almost truthful, my sins there only those of omission. I opened my eyes, the sky full of stars, and a hum of something coming from across the river. Then after a moment the sound of what had been there all night: the click and clack of rail wagons, the scream and screech of metal on metal, the long slow dong dong dong of a train bell. I pulled the blanket up around me and moved about on the hard earth and before I had finished moving I was asleep again. I opened my eyes a moment later and the sky was blue with cream and gold and grey-blue clouds and birds passing. There was a warmth in it, even if the warmth was not yet down along the river or in my bones. It was that cold that made me sit up and face the day.

There was a spider with long legs and a match head body stalking across my hand, and an itchiness around me that made me think I was crawling with ants. I stood up stiff and weary among the sharp wiry bushes and brushed what I could of spiders and crawling things and grit off me. I put my hand to the side of my head, on the tender skin around the cut. I pulled up my shirt. The big purple patch was darker than yesterday. It would mend. I tucked the shirt in again.

As well as the trains now there was a banging and buzzing from somewhere behind me. The lumber mill at work. I could feel the breeze, and with the light and the cool air and the noises I guessed it was about six or six thirty.

To one side a red bridge crossed the river. Just beyond that another river flowed down from the north into this one. It was a pretty enough place and would be hot later, but those high bare brown hills across the water would have had snow on them not long ago. Snow could lie there all year round for all I cared, for I wouldn't be here. I would be in the west, where fruit grew easily and crops were tall and milk cows fed on long thick grass. I would make some patch of that mine, while it was still there to be got, and never be in want or take orders from another man again.

There was a clang clang away on my right. A rail man in dark blue work clothes was walking the line, striking the rails with a long handled hammer and bending to the sound, coming towards me. I rolled up my blanket and put it in my suitcase on top of my shirt and toilet things. I went down to the river and squatted in the bushes. I splashed water on my face and hands, over the bruises and cuts, rubbed water into my stubble and wished I could shave to look respectable. I had another brush at my clothes and put on my hat and walked out of the bushes onto the path.

I stopped. Far off to the east, coming along the path between the river and the rail lines, was a woman. I watched her, straight and slim, walking slowly, steadily, the sun behind her lighting up her pale dress, fluttering through, glowing around her head. She was young and she would be good-looking. A good-looking woman walking slowly along, washed in the bright and warming early light.

I watched her look towards me as she came on, then away to the far banks and the scrubby dry hillsides and not glance in my direction again. As she came closer I saw she wore a broad-collared cream dress that stopped above the ankles, and a cream toque with a spray of feathers. Expensive, luminous clothes. The daughter of a businessman or doctor or lawyer. The wife of such. A woman who went short of nothing. And she was what I had known she would be. She was lovely. She was hoping I wouldn't speak to her, I guessed, down here by the river in the early morning, alone.

And what was she doing here, by the river, so early, and alone?

There was a long slow train beginning to pass her, one of those interminable trains that had been coming through all night, lumber from the coast, reefer cars of beef from the ranch lands in the north, heading for Ontario and Europe and the War, food and supplies for soldiers and the men who sent them there. Suddenly I was embarrassed at her approaching, her looking like that and I in my stubble and slept-in clothes and bloodied head, watching her. I pushed my way through the bushes, crossed the line just ahead of the slow train, and walked over waste land and more tracks and up the slope and into the town. I didn't look back.

I hadn't eaten since the middle of the day before and I had to get something. I went into the first of the little streets of the town. I looked over the fences into back yards and up at windows. Back from the railway lines the houses were bigger and more prosperous, and of brick instead of wood. Ahead I could see the signs of banks and shops. There was the brass name plate of a dentist's surgery on one fine building, and a woman coming out of the doorway to the side. She was well-dressed, with a fur stole, gloves and with a short veil on her hat. The dentist's wife. There was a chance here. She was about to pull the door closed.

'Excuse me, ma'am. Would you be having a coin or two to help a man out? I need something to buy food.' She stiffened; the hand on the door knob froze. 'I'm on my way to the coast to enlist.' That was the thing to say to such women. She turned towards me.

'My own son enlisted here in Kamloops. That was in the first months of the War.' Behind the veil her eyes moved away from me and stayed away. 'Over three years ago, and neither I nor his father have set eyes on him since.'

'My brother in Vernon enlisted right away too, and I came over from Ireland to keep the farm going. But sure the country needs me more.'

The well-dressed woman turned back and closed the door and shook the handle, and came down the three steps to the street and without looking at me said, 'How smooth you are.' She walked away towards the banks and shops. I stood looking after her, then moved towards the wooden shacks and rougher housing. Beyond one garden fence I found a woman, in her forties maybe, pegging out clothes on the line.

'Excuse me, ma'am.' I made the Irish accent deeper. 'Would you be having a little bit of bread maybe, or a cup of tea, for a man down on his luck?' She didn't turn nor look at me but kept on lifting clothes from the basket and holding them to the line and putting in pegs. 'Excuse me, ma'am. Would you be having some food?'

The woman turned. I could see her looking at the cut on my head.

'There's plenty of jobs at the sawmill if you're hungry. There's many a rancher around here would give his arm for a fit man to help on the land.' She shook her head and turned back to the clothes line.

'Thank you anyway, ma'am. I just need to get my strength up a bit before I apply for jobs, for I haven't been well.' I shivered a bit. 'As you can see. But thank you anyway.' I walked away slowly. Then I heard her call.

'Wait there. I'll see what I can do.' She left the basket and went towards the back door of the house. 'And stay there. Don't be coming in. Keep away from the basket.'

She was gone for what seemed a long time, and then she came back. She carried something wrapped in a piece of newspaper. I reached over the fence and took it. It felt like a fat sandwich.

'Thank you, ma'am. This will see me right. Then I can get down to that sawmill.'

She said nothing and there were no smiles from her, and once the sandwich was in my hand she turned away. 'Thank you again, ma'am.' I squeezed the sandwich into my jacket pocket and went on. At a grocery store on a corner of Sixth I bought a loaf from the Mediterranean-looking man behind the counter. As I left another customer came in and called 'Panos' to him, so I took two apples from the barrel at the door.

I walked on up and out towards the road to the west, and sat where I could look down over the town and the sawmill and the junction of the rivers. I tore off some of the bread and ate it with bites of apple. I took out the sandwich. You could be dead any time. No point in saving. I unwrapped the newspaper and in it was two slices of thick bread and plenty of bacon: one of the good sandwiches.

As I sat here with my half loaf and my apple and my cut head, eating the good bacon sandwich, the noise of the town, the mill noises, and the hoots and rumbles and clangs of the trains shuttling in the yard below all seemed far away. The rivers looked so slowly moving from here, glassy and clear. The long shadows on the high brown hills opposite were growing shorter, and the sun had a lot of heat in it. There was a long day ahead, full of unknown things. I felt good.

Something throbbing rapidly had stopped on the road behind me. I twisted round and there was a yellow-spoked wooden carriage wheel, behind that a black-bodied open motor car, and behind that, a woman driver. She had a broad dark hat held on with a silk scarf tied under her chin, a heavy Harris tweed coat and long leather gloves too big for her. She sat looking at me.

'Good morning.' I nodded. I almost said, 'Ma'am'.

The engine throbbed and rumbled on and I sat there, half twisted around, looking at her. A young woman, with money. A businessman or doctor or lawyer's wife or daughter. The woman of the riverside?

'May I take you further along your road?' A precise English voice. I stuffed my half loaf into my case, and stood up and came towards the motor car. There was a bundle of newspapers tied with string, a wooden crate and a small suitcase and four petrol cans in the back.

'Yes.' I fiddled with the door handled, put my case on the floor and got in beside her. There was a clean citrus smell. 'Thank you.' I had never been in a motor car before. She put the engine in gear and took off the handbrake and drove away immediately. She said nothing more for a couple of hundred yards, until we drew up at a gasoline pump outside a general store at a junction on Columbia Street.

'I'm glad you said yes.' There was a quick smile. 'Because you can help me fill these cans. And the one on the back. Where I am going there are not always supplies.'

She stayed where she was and I carried the cans to the pump and a man in dungarees came out and filled the tank and the cans. I carried each can back and replaced it in the rear foot well, and strapped the last can on over the spare wheel. She reached down and paid the man from a small purse, and while he cranked the starting handle I climbed back in. She was brown-eyed, thick dark hair pinned up under that dark hat and, I guessed, almost my own height. I wanted to ask her if she had been walking at the riverside earlier, but then she might have her own reasons for not drawing attention to it, and I said something else.

'I've never seen a woman driving a motor car before.' She nodded once. I'd get her to talk. 'Where did you learn to drive?'

There was no reply, then, 'A long time ago and far far away.'

'I'm sorry.' I suppose I smiled.

'No you're not.' She glanced up at the blue sky and the wisps of clouds, and down again. 'Isn't it lovely just now?'

'The best part of any day. Before things can go wrong.'

'Has something gone wrong?' she asked quickly. She would have seen the cut over my ear. This was my time to give her my hard-luck story and ask for money for a meal or a bed. But there was a sharpness in those brown eyes that made her more than pretty. Suddenly I didn't want to tell any hard luck stories, but I didn't know what else to say either. I shook my head.

'No.' She looked at me, looked away again. I was more sure than ever she was the woman at the riverside. I wanted to say something striking that she would remember me by, as I remembered her. Instead I felt stupid and ordinary, so much younger than her, more than the couple of years that were probably between us. 'We'll always get enough to do us.'

'I can see you are an optimist.' I watched the corners of her mouth and there was a smile there again. When she smiled a little dimple came to her cheek.

'You're smiling because you think I am not sincere.'

'I'm smiling because I know you are.' I liked that exactness in the way she spoke. Her head went back. 'You're Irish,' she said. I watched her move a little, swaying in her seat. 'What are you doing so far from home?' I watched that swaying and wondered what else she might be thinking.

'I'm working my way to the west. When I get there I'm going to enlist.'

She glanced over at me yet again. 'All right.' There was something more serious and heavy-lidded again about those eyes than I had first thought. 'May I ask you where you have been working?'

'I was in the North, in Whitehorse, and around camps there. That's hunting and mining country. But I couldn't stand the cold and I came south to the Okanagan last autumn.'

'What did you do in the Okanagan?'

'What everybody does there. Fruit framing. I ran a team.'

'A manager?'

'Yes, a manager.' I was looking directly at her. I had managed a half dozen wives of itinerant labourers, boxing apples.

'So you have ordered men, then. Did you like fruit farming?'

'I like working out of doors. Yes.'

'You sound like a farmer. More farmer than soldier. Or trapper or miner. An orchardist, definitely.' She glanced away to the side and across the river and up at the dry brown hills and the talus slopes, and I felt she sighed at that. I was looking at her small pale ear, under the hat, under the dark brown hair, the curve of it. I knew now why she had offered me the lift. I was able-bodied and out of work and there was a farm somewhere needing labour.

'And now you are moving on again.' She seemed almost absent-minded.

'West,' I said again.

'From one little place to another. Are jobs hard to get?'

'Not hard.' Here it was about to come.

'I live in a little place. There would be a job there.' I said nothing. 'There would be some management experience called for, so it would be better paid than most. You would save money before you enlist. Do you want to hear more?'

I was being given a lift to a place where I didn't want to go, being offered a job I didn't want to take.

'Sure.'

'All right.' She was looking at me, as if she might change her mind at any moment. 'But I have to tell you: you will end up in the middle of nowhere.'

'I've been there before.' I smiled, and she smiled a little back. 'Where?'

'Footner,' she said.

I shook my head. 'Does the CPR run through?'

She laughed, loudly and openly

'Yes. So you can jump a train and get away any time.'

I laughed suddenly too, for being so obvious.

'I might do that.'

'You might like Footner,' she said.

'Maybe.'

'Perhaps you'll want to stay.'

'Maybe.'

'There's plenty of work, and no one much to do it.'

'OK.' There was plenty of work everywhere.

We travelled on for a while. I watched her hands in the big gloves on the wheel, and got used to sitting up high and feeling the jolts of the road. I was about to ask her about the riverside and the morning when she said, 'This is a Gray-Dort.'

'Yes?'

'Do you like it?'

'Yes.'

'Do you think I have been very patriotic in buying a Canadian motor car?'

'I suppose so.'

We drove on for a little.

'I'm concerned about punctures,' she said. 'Between the ruts and the horseshoe nails.' I looked up at the hills around us, at this country that was nothing but dust and prickly pear cactus and scrawny clumps of couch grass. 'Have you got nothing to say?'

'Maybe I don't know what I should say.'

She laughed, and kept on looking ahead up the road. It was mostly straight but rough in places, and our speed rose and fell all the time. We met wagons and a couple of gigs, some with women behind the whips. Each time the Gray-Dort slowed; each time some wave and shout was exchanged. 'We mustn't frighten the horses,' she said. We met no other motor cars and the road was often empty for mile after mile.

'And you like to work the land,' she said, after a long stretch of empty road. I nodded. Maybe she didn't see me nod, looking up the road for ruts, for she said, loudly and strongly, 'You like to tend the land, to make things grow.'

'It doesn't seem the worst thing to do.'

'Like Candide.'

I had nothing to say about Candide. I was thinking it was bold of her, job or not, taking a strange man into her motor car. She had seen me in my dirty clothes, the cut on me. She wasn't thinking I was something I wasn't. How much did she need labour?

'Did you not sleep well last night?' I asked after a while. There was a pause before she answered.

'Why do you ask?'

'You were out walking so early. Up around the rail yards.' The motor car bumped on further. 'Along the river.'

'Was I?' Then, 'Tell me more about yourself. Tell me about your far distant past. Before you came to Canada.'

'I'm from Richhill in County Armagh.' I had it ready. It was same story I had told in the Okanagan. 'That's apple country. The orchard county of Ireland they call it. Right now in April and May the leaves and the grass will be all wet and everything bright and the air round the house thick with the scent of the blossoms.' For that moment I did think of Ireland, and Dunmaddy, where I was really from, and my family, and the tiny cramped house across the road from the Army stables, the smell of horses and horse dung and straw always in the air. I thought of it with some real longing, and there was a sadness in me, and then I thought of the rest of my life, and I went on with my made-up story.

'I kept thinking like everybody else the War would be over any day. So I left Ireland and crossed the seas to the big new world we had all been reading about in the newspapers: the timber and the plains and the farming. After the War's over I'm coming straight back to the west coast. Have you heard of the Cowichan Valley?'

'Ah. The dream of the west.' She pulled on the wheel and we jolted out of a rut and went on. 'People have been coming to both coasts for centuries. Footner's in the empty heart.'

'I'll do what needs to be done.' She nodded at that and I thought it might be her own philosophy, so I said again, 'Yes. I'll do what needs to be done. What else is there?'

'What you feel should be done, I suppose,' and she turned and examined me and then looked forward again.

'Is that not all the same?' She didn't reply, and I couldn't think of anything else to say. We went on.

CHAPTER TWO

'HOW GOOD IT IS TO HAVE A SQUARE MEAL AGAIN.' I can see Edward, hear him saying this. It was the evening after we had shot the caribou. Lean steaks, half raw, were on tin plates in front of us. 'Even if it means we go a little shy later.'

'Sarah couldn't cook you a better meal,' said Harry. 'You will see her in months, Edward. Months. Then never let any old rogue like me tempt you away from her again.' Had I been Edward I would have split him with the axe. 'May 15th. That's when spring comes. We'll look up, and a whistling swan will be going over, heading north, and we'll know it's spring. But tomorrow we go after the wounded beast. You and I, Edward. We'll get it. We'll get it all right.'

Edward was nodding. I had stomach cramps and hatred, and was giddy with food.

'Is that right, Harry? In those snowdrifts? That animal will have a day and night to be gone. If the wolves don't have it already.'

Neither of them spoke, but Harry threw down the bone he had been sucking. I went back to what I usually did, and said nothing. After a while Harry said,

'And who predicted the return of the caribou in the first place?' He was chewing on a strip of meat. He took it out of his mouth and chopped at it with the knife and put it back in. 'Who said they would be here before the end of the month?' He looked to Edward but Edward kept busy eating. He turned again to me. His hand rose above his head, and the knife came down with a thump and stuck in the wood of the table between us. He leant over the table. His finger, long-nailed, filthy, came up and pointed at me. 'You won't be involved anyway. You and your bad foot. You'll be watching for caribou from the window or the doorstep. Like I planned. That's why the cabin's here.' His dirty fingernail pointed downward. 'Right here, like I planned, on the caribou migration path.'

'Sure.'

'Have I told you...' he turned back to Edward, the subject closed for him, '...the tales I heard at Fort Liard about the Wendigo?'

Later I lay under my blankets and watched him talking to Edward by the stove, the clipped English voices rising and falling. He had taken off his boots and socks and was looking at his feet. He began to rub them, at first with just his fingers and then with caribou fat.

'I have it on my nose as well,' he said. He pointed to his nose and held his face out to Edward. In the light of the candle across the table earlier his nose had looked as always to me. He turned his face from side to side for Edward to see. He dipped his fingers in the dish of caribou fat and rubbed it on his nose.

'Yes,' said Edward. 'A very little.'

Harry was pointing to his nose again. It was glistening now. 'You had need be careful here,' he said. He turned his face towards me, but I had my eyes half-closed as if asleep. 'But I have always held that it's either a feast or a famine. It's not like what we have left behind. It's a feast or a famine, for a certainty, all the time.'

No. It has been a famine, for a certainty, all the time. Because you are a dumb, dangerous, unprepared fool. As I am, to have followed you.

In the morning I was awake first, even though I was staying behind in the cabin. The snow had fallen all through the night. All the energy they had got from the meal the previous evening and from the steaks and liver of breakfast would be burned off struggling through this all day. If they didn't get the caribou it would be a waste they would never make up.

They were awake not long after me, but didn't go out till midday. I know this was Friday, 24th January, for Edward made notes most evenings in a leather-bound notebook he had bought at AH Esch, a commercial stationers in Edmonton. I'd read it sometimes when they were out or sleeping, but all it ever contained were dates and temperatures and details of our failed hunting.

I sat all the short afternoon with the second rifle in what was left of the small stand of black spruce behind the cabin, and watched the frozen river, but there were no more caribou, nor any wolf. No hare, no fox. Harry and Edward staggered back after dark, frozen and weak. Empty-handed. They ate and slept, and there was little inclination to talk from anybody. When we awoke the next morning and were making tea I could see Harry's nose now really had the white and waxy look of frostbite on it. He and Edward were putting sugar in their mugs.

'Are you going after the caribou?'

'Harry thinks it may still be around, the tracks covered in the snow, and all we have to do is stumble across it,' said Edward. I looked at him, wondering how much he believed this.

'You can look at the traplines,' said Harry. 'As best you can.' He had said it gently, as if meant kindly, and not a taunt. 'Or cut what wood you can. I know the trouble you have getting about.'

'Yes.'

'You have to take care of yourself,' said Harry. 'We depend on you.'

I was determining right at that moment to have a great heap of wood ready for when they came back, and a good fire going, and to have covered more of the trapline than usual. Half an hour later I watched them leave. The trapline, as far as I was able to check it, was empty. I had gone so far and was so weak afterwards that I cut hardly any wood. They came back in the dark with nothing.

We were on a height, with the rail line below on the right, and the river beyond that again. Shortly after the river became the wide expanse of a lake. 'Kamloops Lake,' she said. I thought about how she hadn't asked my name. I thought too about those small hands twisting and turning the big wheel, sometimes pulling on the brass levers, and growing warmer inside the leather gloves, and the small feet in the pointed boots on the pedals.

Eventually she turned the motor car off the main road onto a track, bumping down towards the lakeside, and to where small wooden houses were scattered along the shore, some with canoes pulled up in front.

'Savona,' she said. 'Sav-on-ah,' she repeated. 'There's a tea shop here, and I need a cup of tea.' Opposite a little tea room with two tables, both empty, in the shade of the porch, she pulled the car to a halt and got down. 'Come on. Join me.' She pulled off the big leather gloves and threw them into the back of the car. 'Don't you need a drink as well?' and strode off into the tea room. I got down slowly, not sure of myself, for I had no money to spend here. By the time I got to the door she was on her way out again. 'Let's sit here for a while,' she said. She took off the heavy Harris tweed coat and tossed it onto a chair. Beneath was the broad-collared cream dress of the morning. She untied the scarf and took off the hat and tossed it on top of the tweed coat. 'He'll bring out things in a minute.' She worked at her long dark hair where it had been pinned up. 'My name's Sarah,' she said. She held out a hand. 'Sarah Underhill. Mrs Sarah Underhill.' I sat and looked back at her, at the extended hand, at her quiet expression, at how she had strung out this information. I took the hand and shook it.

'Just Jack Butler.'

'Ah, just Jack Butler.'

A man came out with a tray with a tea pot and cups and a saucer with slices of lemon. There was a plate of sandwiches. He put the tray on the table. As he straightened again he looked at me, and kept looking, and then went indoors again.

'Footner is such a small place. But it's got its own charms. It's also a very new place, which is one reason why we are more short of able men than most.' She poured tea into a cup and passed it to me. Those hands were not as pale as I'd imagined them, but square and strong and capable-looking. 'That and the high rate of recruitment. We have been very patriotic. Help yourself to the sandwiches.' It was cool here on the porch, in the shade, the road in front empty, the lake water lapping across the way, two or three canoes far out, men fishing. The sandwiches were salmon and cucumber. I took another. The sky so blue, soft small white clouds crossing it.

'A pretty spot,' she said. The shore here was thick with trees, birch and poplars and aspens as well as pines, but the hills just above were as dry as before. 'You know, when you spoke of enlisting…' she said, and then stopped. 'What did you think I was thinking?'

'What the woman who gave me the white feather in Winnipeg was thinking.'

'You are Irish,' she said. She poked with a spoon at the lemon slice in her black tea. 'Not British.' Maybe Footner would be nothing like the hills around but like this lake shore: a green well-watered place. A second Okanagan. So I told myself.

'Why don't you finish those?' she said, pointing to the sandwiches. 'Footner's a while ahead yet. I would only have to cook you a late luncheon there anyway.'

'You know I can't pay for any of this?'

'I'm not looking for money.' She was looking over my shoulder by now, at the motor car I thought. 'No, indeed not,' she said. We sat on saying nothing more, feeling the cool breeze and the shade and the peace. I ate the last of the sandwiches. She drank another cup of tea with a slice of lemon. Then,

'I've heard a story about the Okanagan, Mr Butler.' When I looked up from the plate her eyes were closed. 'The story of the remittance men who lived around there, and up in the hills, going off to enlist when war was declared, and leaving a can of gasoline in their cabins.' I knew the story she meant. 'Riding to the next cabin, shooting the old horses and lame dogs and burning the place, while a pal did the same at theirs.' She waited. 'Is there any truth in it?'

'I've never seen any burnt cabins around the Okanagan.' Her eyes opened slowly, blinked at the sunlight on the road, on the lake. 'That doesn't mean it didn't happen. But no, I've never seen the burnt cabins.'

'Knowing they would never come back,' she said.

'Would they have been that organised?'

She laughed. 'Probably not. Not the chaps around here anyway. I think it's time to move.' She rose and left money on the table and called 'Thank you, Arnold' into the doorway. She picked up her coat and hat and scarf from the chair. 'Let's get on, then.' I was feeling good after the food and, as no doubt she intended, in her debt. We walked back to the motor car, and she threw the coat and hat and silk scarf over the crate, and while she sat behind the wheel I cranked the handle until the engine caught, and climbed in again.

'You've been shopping. Clothes? New dresses?'

'Oh yes. That's what it is.'

She was so close beside me that at times there was the faint warm scent of her body over the citrus smell, and I liked it. I would look around at the dry scrubby hillsides, and then across at her, and there, always gazing ahead, her and her warming body and those sad and serious eyes. Just after Savona the long lake ended and became a river again, and we rattled across to the other side on an iron bridge.

'My friend the Thompson,' she said. Her head was up, determined.

'It looks a nice river.' It flowed on our left now.

'It's not nice. But it is beautiful.'

'OK.'

'Fast and clear and beautiful and dangerous. It runs like a race horse for mile after mile and well below the benches, so if you get in there's no getting out again.' The motor car bumped on for a minute. 'A sandbank maybe, if you're very lucky. Then down at Lytton it meets the Fraser. A muddy river. You can see the two waters run side by side for hundreds of yards, and then everything becomes dirty. It's what happens.'

'OK.'

'And at last to the sea.'

About an hour later, far off on the left across the Thompson at the foot of pale empty hills, merging into them in the strong sunlight and dust, was a cluster of wooden colonial bungalows and one larger building.

'Footner,' she said. 'My little home.' Yet she didn't look towards it. Beyond the buildings were acreages of young green trees, drifts of white scattered over them, more green land further off, but outside these fenced squares and rectangles there was nothing that wasn't dull and lifeless. Her right hand rose, finger pointing upward. 'Our irrigation system,' she said. Running parallel with the road but high above us was a long, brown wooden flume, raised on piles, disappearing, coming into view again.

'Yes.'

The flume came down ahead of us, went under the road and on towards the river.

'It flows from Deadmans Creek twenty miles back in the hills. A pipe takes it over the Thompson.' If I needed any confirmation about Footner this was it. I looked at her, trying to read her expression, but there was only her steady gaze on the road ahead. 'I get a little water from Jimmie Creek. It runs through my place. But the town needs the flume.'

'Twenty miles?'

'Yes.' It was firm and final. She turned onto a track on the left, and we wound our way down towards the river. There was a sharp turn to the left, and ahead a single lane iron bridge across the Thompson. Just before the bridge she pulled the Gray-Dort into the side and stopped. She got out and took the Harris tweed coat and the hat and scarf and gloves and put them all on again and got back in and drove across the bridge. We went up around a tight bend on the other side, climbing all the time, and I could see her struggle with the wheel and then the road levelled out. The river was far below us, two hundred feet or more, and all around the dust and prickly pear cactus and scrawny clumps of couch grass.

Then the first small orchards, the trees young and widely spaced, and the first half dozen bungalows, all along one side of the road, facing the river. A few of the houses were shut up, with boards fixed across the windows. We passed more buildings, some with signs for a general store, a butcher's, a draper's. The streets were deserted.

To the left, overlooking the river, was the large building of two storeys, a long balcony on white pillars running from wing to wing. An elderly man, well-dressed and with a cane, stood in the doorway, his head turning from side to side as if listening. 'The Hotel,' said Mrs Underhill, indicating with a nod. 'And Major Sidgwick, our oldest resident.' She squeezed the big rubber bulb of the horn and the old man, upright and heavily moustachioed, waved. 'The Hotel, like 'just' Jack Butler, is 'just' the Hotel. Miss Eleanor Weir is the manager. Last month her brother Gordon was posthumously awarded the Victoria Cross.'

A hundred yards away across the junction, facing the Hotel, were the sturdy-looking cabins and offices of a rail station, with a short platform and a guard's van in a siding. A man in railway uniform sat on a chair and watched us pass.

'The Canadian Pacific Railway,' she said. 'When we want to send our apples away on a train we have no difficulties. Most of the time.' She pulled the motor to a halt outside a house a little larger than the others and with sheds and a small barn with the double doors wide open. 'So I hope you have noticed what a well-equipped little town you have arrived in. Help me with the crate.'

I got down and tugged on an end. 'You can't lift that. It's too heavy.'

'Take an end, Mr Butler.' The imperative edge in that English voice. 'I lifted it in after all.' Between us we manhandled it out of the back seat and onto the ground. She was flushed by then, under that coat and hat and big gloves.

'Wait.' A burly man of about fifty, putting on his jacket, hurrying out. 'Lift nothing more, Mrs Underhill.' I thought at first he too was English, but there was a trace of something else there. 'If you let me take this end…' He was bending, getting his hands underneath the crate. I watched him for a moment and then picked up the other end. 'Into the garage will do.' He backed away in the direction of the small barn and I followed him. I could hear something metallic rattle and clang in the crate.

'Mr Dunae.' Mrs Underhill had come in behind us. 'May I introduce Mr Jack Butler. All the way from Ireland.'

'Yes?' Mr Dunae, his face red, stood getting his breath back.

'From County Armagh, in Ireland,' she said.

'Yes,' said Mr Dunae. He held a handkerchief, and wiped his palm on it and held out the hand. 'How do you do?' I shook the hand.

'Armagh being known as "the orchard county of Ireland", Mr Dunae,' said Mrs Underhill. Mr Dunae's grip on my hand tightened.

'Aahh,' he said. He shook my hand once more. 'The orchard county of Ireland. Of course. That would be apple orchards?'

'Mostly apples. Some pears.'

'And he has been managing teams in the Okanagan,' said Mrs Underhill.

'Aahh,' said Mr Dunae again.

'Mr Charles Dunae is the present manager of Footner.'

The manager. Footner was what I had thought it was from the orchards, the flume, the uniformity of the houses. A ready-built township sold sight-unseen to trusting idiots in England. There would be no Irish or Welsh or Scots here. No Canadians either.

'This is a little town with prospects, and I'm sure there is something here for you,' said Mr Dunae. He was American. An American who sounded English.

'Perhaps you and Mr Dunae would like to have a little chat, Mr Butler?'

'Tomorrow, Mrs Underhill. Would that do? When you've told me more about the town?'

'Whatever suits you best,' said Mrs Underhill. 'Mr Butler and I shall be back in the morning, Mr Dunae.' How wrong she was. 'I'll bring your Gray-Dort back this evening, and we can settle bills then, if that's all right.'

'Keep her till the morning. When you are coming in anyway. Thank you for picking it up. There were no problems?'

'Repaired and ready. We shall see you tomorrow.'

We got back in the motor car and moved off again. I'd have supper and a place to sleep and breakfast before I let her know that I didn't want a job here. She pulled the motor car to a halt at a house on the right. 'Have to pick up something this time,' she said, and stepped down and swept off up the garden path to the door and knocked once and walked in. In moments she was out again, carrying a fox terrier, a young woman with her. The young woman looked at me for a moment. They exclaimed and hugged, the dog caught between them, and separated. Mrs Underhill came back to the car, holding the dog up towards me.

'Meet my eldest child,' she said. 'My only child. Not Mrs Susan Fellowes, who is my friend. Hector. Though not in the least warlike in nature. A pushover, aren't you old dog?' She pushed the dog into my arms. 'Hold him tight. He doesn't know you and he'll be off.' She climbed up and pulled out into the road again, and past more bungalows, as identical as the others, some again empty looking. Beyond the bungalows, over the rail tracks where the land rose up into the hills, was a long low rough cabin. Several Chinese workmen stood outside or sat on stools, watching us pass.

The dog, black and tan and wiry haired, was licking my face, and Mrs Underhill kept turning to watch as she drove.

'Ah. Hector likes you. Has he made a good choice?'

'I'm not sure.' The dog was licking furiously at my ear.

She laughed. 'Neither am I.'

The road got rougher, dropping down towards the river. We forded a tiny stony stream, the bunch grass a little greener along it. 'The Jimmie,' she said. At the house at the end of the track, in style and size and newness like all the others, she pulled the motor car to a stop. We sat there, the engine cooling and ticking. Around us spread a few acres of apple trees, like all the others six or seven years old at most. Ahead was a shed and a small empty corral, but there was no barn or any of the outbuildings that might be expected on a farm. I let go of the dog and he leaped to the ground.

'Good to be home, Hector, eh?' she said. 'I would never go far without my Hector.' She got down, picked up the bundle of newspapers from the back seat, and walked towards the house. She pulled off her gloves and raised the edge of a terracotta pot of geraniums, little tightly-rolled scarlet flowers about to open. She took a key from underneath the pot. 'Now you know all my secrets,' she said, looking up at me. She unlocked the door. 'Why don't you dismount from that thing? And take the last package with you. Please.' I followed her into a short hallway with a vaulted ceiling, fifteen or sixteen feet high, right to the roof. On the left a hall table and framed English hunting prints, and two doors, one, to a bathroom, open. I set my suitcase by the bathroom door. On the right a bedroom, a too-large-for-this-house double bed with an ornate darkwood headboard, wardrobe and dressing table. Past that an open kitchen. She dropped the newspapers on the kitchen table. 'Could you put that there?' she said, pointing beside it. The package clanked as I put it down.

There was another door ahead of us, above which hung the head of an antelope, or some other animal that had never walked in these parts. She opened the door and with a wave of her hand showed me into a room with a desk and a tall brass lamp and comfortable leather armchairs. There was a thick red rug on the stained floorboards in front of the fireplace, and a smell of wood polish in the air.

'The parlour,' she said. 'There are English and Canadian newspapers in the rack by the desk. Out of date, of course. But now we have a new supply.' Her eyes widened and she smiled again, pleased. 'I'll make tea.' I was looking at the low bookcases around the walls. Silverware on top: candlesticks, a vase, bowls, snuff boxes, an ash tray in the shape of a horseshoe. 'Edward's family things.' She had noticed me looking. 'Edward's my husband.'

I waited to hear what regiment he was with, and his rank, and where in France he was serving, but she was already walking away, untying her scarf. 'And you may wash up, of course.' I looked around at the silver for another minute and followed her back into the kitchen. The package had been torn open and canned foods, corned beef, salmon, peaches, jam, spread around on the table. Hector stood at her feet, looking up. 'I'll wash my hands.' She nodded.

I took my suitcase into the bathroom with me. There was an enamel bath and a wash basin. I filled the basin with cold water from a jug. I used her soap and clean flannel and towel and washed my hands and face. The cloths were marked when I finished. I opened the suitcase and changed my shirt. There was the half loaf, crumbling away over my clothes. I closed the case again. When I came out of the bathroom there was a smell of paraffin from the stove.

'Splendid,' she said on seeing me. I couldn't have been very different. 'Tea and cake.'

The table was laid out with the tea things and a fruit cake. There was a bowl of apples. She sat across from me and poured a cup of tea.

'Thank you. All this is very kind.'

'I should have brought bread with me. But we have a bakery here that opens for a few hours each morning.'

'Excuse me.' I stood up and went to the case and opened it and took out my half loaf. I held it up, the used end crumbling away from where I had torn lumps off that morning. She sat stiff-backed and immobile and watching me, and I realized what I was doing: offering her my mangled bread. I felt my face go red. 'It's fresh. Or it was earlier.' I turned it from side to side as I spoke and more bits fell off. When I looked next she was laughing. I put the half loaf back in the case.

'No. No. Bring it here.' Her hand reached out. 'Thank you for your contribution to the meal, Mr Butler. I'll trim your loaf a little and it will be fine.' I gave her the loaf and she trimmed the end and cut slices and brought them and a butter dish back to the table.

'Now: let us have our tea before it is cold.' She was buttering one of the slices of bread as she spoke. She took a large apple and began to cut it up into wedges and put some on my plate.

I was looking at the window as if what was outside was interesting but it was only the side of the shed and some of the closer young apple trees. She was looking at me, and then down at her plate, and then at me again. She cut a piece of apple and passed it to the dog and watched him eat. I felt we were waiting for something. I spoke instead.

'The trees.'

'Yes?'

'What types of trees have you planted out there?'

'Jonathons.'

'You didn't want Rome Beautys, or Wealthys?'

She shook her head. 'We were in a hurry.'

'I see, Mrs Underhill.' I sat on, not drinking my tea and not looking at her either. 'This is very nice.' I cleared my throat. 'But I can't…'

'I think you know what Footner is,' she said. 'In this case run by BCHEC: the British Columbia Horticultural Enterprise Company.'

'Yes. That…'

'Let me tell you more about it. By the end of that August when war was declared forty three of the men of Footner had already enlisted.' I was nodding. I had heard tales like this before. 'By the end of the first year over a hundred and twenty men were gone. That was almost every man of working age we had. Footner, as I said, has been very patriotic. And other men have left since, to work as civil servants, or in some support capacity.' She stopped. 'And many wives have gone. Children have gone. All until the War is over.'

I wanted to say this right. 'I can see your problem. But there is nothing I can do about that.' Why wasn't I waiting till morning to just slip away as I had always intended? 'I can't do the work of a hundred men.'

'The hundred men did not do the work of a hundred men. You know that also.'

'Mrs Underhill…'

'You can help keep the flume operating. You can run a team of Chinese workers. As long as there is irrigation the trees will survive somehow.' I sat there thinking of the scorching sun, the hard winters. The soil would be thin out there, inches of dust over rock. 'The Okanagan is flourishing. You know that. We can make a go of it here too, once the War is over and the men are back.' I was looking at my plate with the bread and butter and already darkening wedges of apple, and my hands flat on the tablecloth either side of my plate. Did she believe any of this?

'Mrs Underhill, maybe you should think of…'

'Others might have left their land and walked away. I'm not walking away. I can't afford to. Charles Dunae will pay you as well as you would get anywhere. You can sleep in the bunkhouse here, and work on the flume for any of the town who care any more. I will give you breakfast and dinner, and in return you do a few of the jobs that are too heavy for me alone.'

I looked across the table top and there were her hands on the table beside her plate also.

'Any of the town who care any more?'

'I care.' She was looking back at me. Oddly, she was smiling. 'There's no hurry. Go back to the parlour with a cup of tea while I tidy up in here. Take a *Times* or a *Globe* with you.' I shook my head and said nothing. I was looking at the dimple in the cheek when she smiled, the brown eyes and the heavy serious eyelids. 'There's no hurry about anything,' she said. I got to my feet and went back to the parlour.

I should have picked up my suitcase there and then and thanked her for the food and left Footner and her and her problems and never thought of any of them again. Maybe if she had said 'We can't afford to' instead of 'I can't afford to' I would have. But I didn't. I thought of her struggling on her own, smiling while she knew her world was all shot to hell, and told myself I could still leave in the morning.

Much later, at a time when I was sure I would stay on and on here, she said something else about this farm. I'd asked her, in those good days, how she had been so lucky as to have the one house in Footner that was not readily visible from most of the others.

'I looked at them and thought: which one of these will be best for sneaking my lover into?' She had spoken quickly. 'That's the one I told Edward to buy,' and then she laughed. 'I am joking.' Later she said: 'Edward chose it for Jimmie Creek and the most sheltered orchards,' but it was too late then.

CHAPTER THREE

I KEPT THE RIFLE USUALLY LEFT WITH ME, the 25-35 Savage, clean, wanting to use it. I had never seen Harry clean the short magazine Lee-Enfield Mark III, the standard rifle of the infantry, that he carried. I picked it up. I could hardly see up the barrel for filth, and the bolt action screeched for lack of oil. I took it apart on the table, cleaned it, pulled it through, greased it with fox fat, and reassembled it. When I looked up Harry was awake and watching me.

'Thank you,' he said. His lips had taken on a chewed, blackened look. He lay quietly for a while under his blankets. 'I didn't ask you to do that.'

'You take no care of your weapon.' The great hunter of the North.

'I could see my .303 was in good hands.' I let it pass. Then, 'I wonder what you are thinking?' That surprised me, but I let it pass too. 'So. I have a new plan. We'll search the area around the cabin for the bones and remains we threw away in the early winter. I can recall where we put these things. Even under all the snow. I have the recollection of the Indian and the squirrel for that.'

He went out later and came back without finding any of the dumps. Another day without food.

On February 12th I found a fox in one of the traps. It made me think maybe Harry had not put them in such a bad position after all, until I thought again of all the other useless walks along this same trapline. Back at the cabin, the fox cut into pieces, I took stock of the rest of our food supplies. We had forty cups of flour and about twenty pounds of sugar, and more tea than we could face on empty stomachs. For meat, once the fox was eaten, there were four caribou hides and a few wolverine hides we had been using to keep out drafts.

I found two hares in the trapline soon after, and that kept us alive for one more week. There was no talk now of the herds of caribou or the plentiful wolves that followed them.

One evening, sorting again through bones, even Edward exclaimed, 'This game of always being short of grub is hell.' Then, shortly after, 'I hope Sarah is all right.'

'You are a lucky man, Edward.' Harry, across the table. 'If I have a regret about any of this it's that I took you away from her.' When I looked Edward was sitting silently, glumly. How could Harry talk like this? How could Edward let him? 'What would she be saying about this situation now, eh?' Edward looked too tired to respond. 'She would say: Let's do it,' said Harry. 'What she always says. Yes. Let's just do it.'

No. Let's get on with it. That's what she says. I rose and left them and their thoughts of Sarah, and began to search for the dumps from our now so profligate-seeming autumn and early winter. Edward came out shortly after, and half an hour later he had scraped away snow and found fox bones.

That was on the 22nd of February. In Footner the apple trees were ready to prune. Here the temperature scribbled in pencil in Edward's notebook was -29°F. When I read these entries at first I thought it might help me see that time was indeed passing, that one day spring would come, that we would pull thorough. It did nothing but show me how slowly the days passed, how it grew colder, but I kept reading them, turning the knife in myself further: I didn't have to be here. I had chosen this. As Edward had chosen it.

THURSDAY, 25TH APRIL 1918

I lay awake, looking at the boards of the low ceiling. From far away came the clang clang clang of a train bell, and then it stopped. There was a little light in the sky. Through the window I could see the tops of young apple trees. I guessed it was about five o'clock. Soon, in her bedroom, the sunlight would shine on the curlicues along the top of the big dark wood wardrobe. It would move down to her dressing table. To the heavy carved head of her bed. It would shine in her eyes, and then she would awake. I lay on, thinking about her, listening to my breathing, watching the light grow.

While there was still time, before she awoke, I had to rise and dress and check if the house door was unlocked. This was the countryside. Naïve Canadian countryside. It would be unlocked. I would take all the food I could carry and slip out again. Maybe something else. Small things. I would jump a train to the west. I might have to go into town for that. When I opened the shed door there was a woof from Hector. He stood on the porch, ears pricked, a wondering look about him, and then came forward, tail wagging.

'Stay. Stay.'

I stroked him, and tried the door. Of course it opened. I stepped into the hall, and stood there listening, but all was silent. Her bedroom door was ajar. I took three, four steps along the hall, and looked through. There was her dressing gown on the floor where she had thrown it the night before. Her dress draped over a chair. A wicker linen basket. On the dressing table her hair brush, a hand mirror, little tongs and files and other woman's things. These she would know and use when she rose, before she found I was gone and wasn't taking her job. I pushed the door open another foot, waiting for the creak, but none came and now I could see the bed and her in it.

She was lying on her side, turned towards the window, rich dark hair tousled on the pillow. In the early light and shadows I could see only part of her face. A hand was raised and lay on the pillow close to her cheek. I could see a naked pale shoulder where the shadowy blue nightdress had slipped down.

I pulled the door over again. I stepped quietly along to the kitchen. The newspapers were spread across the table. I opened the cupboards where she had stored the things from the package the night before. Tinned salmon, corned beef, jars of Frank Cooper's marmalade. Crackers. Cheese. Plenty.

But instead of taking anything I walked back into the hall. I wasn't sure what I was looking for. Maybe something more valuable. I opened the first door on the right. A dining room, with a long table and six chairs and a sideboard, all again in the dark mahogany of the bedroom, all again made for a house larger and older than this one. The smells of fresh bare softwood and often-polished hardwood. I had been in houses like this before, each for a little while, all along the plains and into the mountains. I tried another door off the dining room. A small room: by the heaps of clothing piled on the bed, an unused guest bedroom. I went back towards the kitchen, but instead of picking up the groceries I again went to the only other door I had not opened, the one opposite her bedroom.

It was as big as the parlour. Another half dozen African or Indian animal heads on the walls. A cricket bat and pads stood by the door, a bag of golf clubs propped up next to them. A tennis racquet in a press lay on the floor. Fishing rods in racks. A sportsman would be along any minute. Three and a half years late. There were the comfortable leather chairs I had expected, and beside one of the chairs a small table with an ashtray and a rack of briar pipes and an ivory tusk spills holder. Along the top of the one bookcase were photographs of young men in cricket whites, in ties and waistcoats playing leap-frog in a field, standing straw-hatted in a punt. Older men, all holding rifles, clustered around a fallen lion. Beneath the photographs were John Wisden's cricketers' almanacs, volumes of Jerome K Jerome and Conan Doyle, *Diary of a Nobody* and *Vice Versa*. I took down a Wisden and thumbed through it, looking at the incomprehensible figures. I put it back and stood there, listening to the creaks of the wooden walls, the still-tightening pine of the floor boards, looking from the cricket pads to the golf clubs, and out through the two large windows to the still-grey orchards and blue-grey talus slopes.

On the right was an upright piano. On the piano were two more photographs, in matching dark wood frames. A younger looking Sarah, in an English garden, holding up a black spaniel, smiling. In the other a slim dark-haired man standing in front of a summer house, in hunting costume, a whip in one hand, his riding hat in the other. The sun on what looked like a late autumn day threw his shadow behind him as he squinted slightly and smiled.

'Wheathampstead, Hertfordshire,' said a voice behind me. I turned. She was standing there, the dressing gown closed tightly across her, long dark hair fixed behind her. 'Edward was a terrible huntsman really. He just enjoyed riding around the lanes for an afternoon, and coming in for a good tea.'

She came forward and stood close to me, looking intently at the photograph. There was a sudden warmth beside me in this room with its cool dead air of morning. She stood on, looking at the photograph, serious and silent.

'Tell me about him.' To deflect attention.

'We grew up together,' she said. 'Like brother and sister.'

'Yes?'

Her head bent to the side with a quick movement. How familiar already that movement, that straight back, the waving hair. She continued to look at the photograph.

'Our families were neighbours. When I was a child I would walk through onto their property and there he would be, running away from his governess, or chasing his black Labrador. We would steal apples together. I would go into his house and he into mine and explore empty rooms, and make up stories in them.'

I too was looking at the face of the man in the photograph. A face she had seen in Wheathampstead while I was a child in Ireland, in play, later in evenings across the fireside in this room, and in love making. All this life of hers that was nothing to do with me. I was inhaling the warmth of her, the sense of quiet and rest and sleep. I could see her naked feet. The fingers of one hand holding the edge of the dressing gown. 'We would swim in the Lea in summer. His father had a tree house built, and we would play in it.' She stopped.

'Tell me more.' She looked away from the photograph and up at me.

'Perhaps you had better get on,' she said. 'Take some things from the kitchen, won't you?'

'I was awake. I thought you would be up and about and making tea. I had no idea it was so early.' She said nothing. 'I'll go outside again.' I suddenly so much wanted to make this life of hers something to do with me. 'Until later. Then maybe we can talk about what I should say to Mr Dunae.'

She put her hands in the pockets of the dressing gown and stood looking at me.

'You want that?'

'Yes. And whatever jobs I'm needed for here.'

'All right. And, Mr Butler…'

'Yes?'

'Don't just walk in.'

'No.'

'Come back in half an hour. I'll have made pan bread.'

I walked away at that, towards the door and the yard and the dog and the wooden shed she called the bunkhouse.

MONDAY, 29TH APRIL 1918

'The main thing is the flume.'

Right across the hillside above us and on distant hillsides ran the wooden trough. At places it was on the ground, at others held up on props. Mr Dunae's hand came down again and into the jacket pocket of his good, English-cut, fine tweed suit. 'The main thing is always the flume. You can see leaks from here.' We stood and looked at the silver trickles in the sunlight. 'Multiply that by twenty miles and there's a lot of water lost by the time we reach Footner. Wang Chi and the boys have been working steadily on this since last year. If you spend a while with them and see the sort of thing that has to be done, then we can move you onto the piping and channels into town and through the orchards.'

I nodded to Wang Chi, to be friendly. I kept looking at Wang Chi, whose job I had taken, and he looked rather disinterestedly back, which I took to be a good thing. The 'boys', four other Chinese men, all probably in their forties and fifties, stood around with saws and hammers and bags of nails, and looked the other way.

'So I'll leave you to it now. I'll see you at some point tomorrow and you can give me your impressions. So: pip pip.'

With that he turned and crunched off down the hillside and over the prickly pear to where the Gray-Dort was parked on the roadside. Pip pip. I turned back to Wang Chi.

'Well. No time to waste. Let's get on.'

I had no idea what to do, except be the works manager, so I led the way up to the flume. We stopped where a trickle showed on the dark warped thin pine.

'Who is the best at fixing these leaks?' I asked Wang Chi. He shrugged.

'We all fix them.'

'All right. Who would you order to fix this?'

He said something which I did not understand.

'What?'

'John,' he said.

'John?'

Wang Chi pointed.

'Who are the others?'

'Matthew. Simon. James.' His finger came down again. In Footner they were John, Matthew, Simon and James. And Wang Chi.

'Well. Let's work along the flume. I will work with you and I will also inspect your work. All right?' Wang Chi nodded once, and waited. 'Well, tell them.' He told them something, and the others began to scatter along the flume. 'And give me a hammer and nails.'

And so my work in Footner began. In places accessible from the road planks had been heaped up, and someone would go down at times and carry up wood. I came after them along the flume, hammering in the odd nail, sometimes sawing a new piece to length and adding it to the patchwork already there. Sometimes one of the props would have to be righted and strengthened. I could see myself and the 'boys' doing this work until kingdom come. I didn't have a lot to say to them, and they had nothing at all to say to me.

About what I guessed was noon the men downed their tools. I heard Wang Chi call to them, and then look at me. I nodded. He called to them again and they went back to where they had left their bundles. I sat on the edge of the flume, keeping out of the prickly pear and ants. They sat on rocks down the hillside where I could watch them. We all had something wrapped up to eat. I had a couple of sandwiches and an apple and a bottle of cold tea. The others took out wicker boxes and removed the lids and began to eat intricate-looking things with chopsticks. They had been silent all morning and now talked rapidly and quietly. Sometimes they would laugh, also quietly. There was a warm, dry smell in the air from where we had stomped through the early sage with our boots, and there was the crackle and chirp of insects and birds around us, and now and then the high, quiet laughter.

At the end of the day I would go back to Mrs Underhill's shed. The bunkhouse. I would wash up in the basin at the door. I would eat an evening meal. I would carry water in buckets from the Jimmie to the water tank. Maybe she would play that piano for me. It would work out. In the heat and the scents of the earth I was half asleep. There was a humming. A motor car down on the road, a motor car coming from Footner. A woman in the driver's seat, in a pale dress, shimmering in the sun. How she shimmered. Her dog sat in the front beside her. The seat I had sat in, beside her. She stopped the car, looked towards me, smiled, started towards me. 'Sarah.' She was golden, with the sun on her dress. 'Sarah.' I had said it aloud. There was no motor car on the road. No Sarah. I got to my feet. Below me the men were talking and smoking cigarettes and paying no attention.

In the afternoon it got cloudy, and cooler, and looked like rain, but no rain fell. At some point the men downed tools again and went back to their bundles.

'Time for a break,' I called.

They ate what was left of their food. I ate the crusts of my bread and thought about what Mrs Underhill might be like under that shimmering dress. Then I thought about what I should be doing for myself, and forgot about her.

After a while the men went back to work. Later again, as the sun started to go lower in the grey clouds, they began to pack up and move off down the hillside. Then Wang Chi called something to them and they stopped and waited. This time they were all looking towards me.

I called Wang Chi over.

'It's quitting time, Wang Chi. You and the boys go home.'

'Yes, boss.'

He called to the others, and they started off again down the hillside. I hadn't seen anything change on their expressions. I liked that. I waited until they were gone, and followed them back down to the Government Bridge and towards Footner. Charles Dunae had driven us all out, but no one had driven us home. As I passed the CPR depot two rail men in dark blue uniforms were sitting out on the bench, and another, in coveralls, came out of the cabin. One of them waved and I waved back. Over the rail tracks Wang Chi and his boys and other Chinese were cooking on a fire outside the long low rough cabin. They watched me pass too, but there was no waving.

As I turned the corner of the house Hector came running from the back, barking, and then stopped on seeing me. I went on. There were two horses now in the small corral. At the clothes line from the house to the shed Mrs Underhill was unpegging washing. She turned, a peg in her mouth. She removed the peg.

'There you are. How was your first day?' She seemed happy and easy. Her smile stayed there, and she bent to the basket at her feet, and straightened again. 'I've made a little dinner. I tried to time it so we could eat together.'

'That's very good of you.'

'I'm not disinterested. You know that. I've got our horse Cap over from the Fellowes' place, and there's Sam, a good cayuse, for you. So no more walking to and from work.'

I looked down at the state of my work clothes, the dirt on my hands, the feel of the grit on my face and in my teeth. The work hadn't been heavy, but dirty and sweaty.

'I'll go and wash, Mrs Underhill.' Then, as I moved away, she called.

'Jack.'

I turned. She was holding a peg in one hand, some small item of clothing in the other. She was smiling, but there was that stillness and seriousness about her. 'I think you shall be a great asset here. What do you think, Hector?' Then she bent suddenly and patted the dog's head with the hand that held the clothes peg, and straightened and got on with taking in the clothes.

I stood looking at her back as she worked. Then, hungry for my meal, looking forward to sitting at the table with her, I walked to the door of the bunkhouse and plunged my hands into the basin of water there. Already I felt like I had done this before, and would do it many times again. I wasn't sure if that was a good feeling or not.

SATURDAY, 11TH MAY 1918

'It's a splendid evening,' said Mrs Underhill. 'And as we know, chances of rain are slight.' We were walking into town under the hard bright starlight, the earth of the road pale in front of us. '*Nil desperandum*,' she said as we passed the first houses. 'No need for the glum look. You are looking very smart in Edward's suit. Miss Weir will be very glad to meet you.'

'I won't know anybody.' Every day I had gone to work on the flume and come straight back to the house.

'Jack, since coming here, who have you spoken to?'

'Charles Dunae, the Chinese, who didn't reply, old Willie the wagon driver, and you, Mrs Underhill.'

'Oh.'

'Maybe I don't want to know anybody.'

'You cheerful chap.'

At the Hotel all the lights were on, and a piano, violin and clarinet were playing My Chocolate Soldier Sammy Boy. Across the open ground at the CPR depot two rail men sat under an oil lamp, smoking and watching the Hotel. On the long balcony above the entrance, against the glow from the windows, figures were passing. 'Miss Weir has already said she is looking forward to meeting the great asset I managed to inveigle into coming to Footner. Or words to that effect. You should have taken yourself to the Hotel ages ago.'

'Before the War I wouldn't have been allowed into Miss Weir's Hotel.'

'Oh there wasn't room for half the people who wanted to use the Hotel in those days.' How quickly she had spoken. 'Good evening, Mrs Hudson.'

'A lovely evening,' said Mrs Hudson. On her left arm was a black armband.

'Now: put your smile on, Jack. We are almost there. Good evening, Mrs Morrison. Mrs Bennie and Isa.'

'Good evening. Splendid evening.'

'Oh, yes,' said Mrs Underhill. 'Splendid.' She strode ahead up the steps and unto the porch. A woman in her late thirties, in a dark dress, again with a black armband, her hair pulled back, her mouth in a tight smile, waited by the door of the dining room.

'Good evening, Miss Weir,' said Mrs Underhill.

'Mrs Underhill. And her escort.' How fixed and sour that smile was. On the wall behind Miss Weir hung a portrait photograph of a young man, dark hair swept back, eyes rather widely open. The photograph was draped in black crepe ribbon. Gordon Weir, then.

'Mr Jack Butler, Miss Weir. My aide-de-camp. I hear you have not yet met.'

'Indeed.' Miss Weir's hand came out. Her grip was slight and dry. 'Mr Butler.' Below the portrait photograph was a framed map of western Europe, little paper flags in place. Union Flags, red, white and blue tricolours, Stars and Stripes, the red of India and South Africa and Canada, the blue of Australia, the black, white and red of Germany.

'Good evening, Miss Weir.' I thought about her dead brother with his Victoria Cross. I thought about how those flags wouldn't have moved much in the past three and a half years. I stood there with nothing to say to her.

'This was of course a splendid idea of yours, Mrs Underhill,' said Miss Weir. 'And very fitting.'

'We must find our table, Miss Weir. Mustn't keep them waiting.'

'The tide is most definitely on the turn in Europe, Mrs Underhill,' said Miss Weir. 'The stalemate broken,' but she was already looking past us. 'Mr Jameson. Welcome to this evening.' A young man, limping heavily, was behind us. Mrs Underhill took my elbow and steered me between the tables of the dining room. I didn't ask what the splendid idea was. There were elderly men and women and a few younger women spread around these tables in fours and sixes. There was no sign of old Willie or any of the CPR men. There was a Chinese waiter. It was John, from the flume.

'Mrs Dunae,' called Mrs Underhill. 'Your husband will be along?' The woman nodded. We kept walking. 'Good evening, Mrs Scott. Good evening, Mrs Trip.' Mrs Underhill nodded to others. 'There,' she said, leaning towards me. At a table at the top of the room, not far from the three women with the piano, violin and clarinet, sat Mrs Susan Fellowes. Old Major Sidgwick was beside her. Mrs Fellowes waved, Major Sidgwick sat facing ahead. We made our way towards them. There was a carriage clock nearby on a small side table.

'Bought by subscription for Major Sidgwick, and brought across from the station today by Willie,' said Mrs Underhill quietly as we came closer.

'Your splendid idea?'

'Yes. Now a man in his mid eighties will be able to hear every quarter and half hour go by. If you think that is a splendid idea.' She shook her head. We were almost at the table.

'Major Sidgwick,' said Mrs Underhill. 'May I introduce a young man who combines being my lodger, my jack of all trades, and Mr Dunae's new right-hand man? Mr Jack Butler.'

'Sir,' said the old man. His right hand went out approximately in my direction, but his expression was unchanged. He was blind. 'I have heard of you and your works.' I put my hand into his.

'How do you do, sir.'

'Ah. Of course. The Irish chap,' said the Major. 'Welcome to Footner. Not a lot of young men around these days. I hope it won't be boring for you.'

'No, sir. I have plenty to do.'

'There is a lot to do, Major,' said Mrs Underhill. 'And Susan: you have glimpsed but not met Mr Butler.'

'Jack.' We shook hands. She was pretty and fair haired and smiling.

'Sit, Jack,' said Susan Fellowes. 'The Major was just about to tell one of his famous anecdotes.'

'Oh no.' The old man's head shook. 'No.' A glass of brandy sat in front of him. His hand went out and unerringly closed around it. 'I wasn't. You've heard all my stories, anyway. I've told you about my part in Jameson's Raid, haven't I?' He drank half the brandy swiftly. 'Not that Jameson who delivers the telegrams and newspapers. Not him. The Boer War Jameson.' His head turned about, trying to find me. The women were starting to laugh.

'I haven't heard it, sir.' It was what I thought was expected.

'Well, I wasn't in it,' came the retort. 'I'm far too old. What are you thinking?' Both women were laughing openly now. 'Damned bad idea from the start. Always thought so. They were a bunch of idiots.'

'I told you the Major was famous for his anecdotes,' said Susan. She was a pretty young woman who laughed readily. Most men would have liked her. I liked her.

'The Major has a wonderful past, and a wonderful military record, if a little earlier than Jameson's Raid,' said Mrs Underhill. 'He would have a fund of great stories, were he a man to boast of them, which he is not.'

47

The sound of the piano, violin and clarinet died away. The sound of voices began to fall, and there was the sense that we were waiting.

'Mr Dunae,' said Susan. 'At last.' My boss was making his way towards our table. Everybody was watching him. Applause broke out and two or three of the men cheered.

'So why are we here?' said the Major. 'I can't remember the occasion. Have I been told?' He looked puzzled.

'Soon, Major,' said Mrs Underhill.

Mr Dunae was smiling. He stopped by our table.

'May I have your attention, please?' he called, unnecessarily. 'I hope you have all been enjoying yourselves so far tonight. I saw one or two on the balcony earlier who certainly had...' He waited for the ripple of laughter to subside. Mrs Underhill leant towards me.

'Miss Weir considers Prohibition a law only for Canadians.'

'We are here tonight to honour our oldest and most distinguished resident,' Mr Dunae went on. The Major beside me murmured something. 'This, tonight, is his birthday. I hope you don't mind if I say it is your eighty-fourth, Major Sidgwick. As your son, the renowned Captain Sidgwick, is off bravely serving his country this, I am sure, happy event has been organised by the ladies on either side of you...'

I leant back in my seat. I looked from Susan Fellowes on one side of me to Mrs Underhill on the other: two attractive young women doing a kind thing for an old man. There were worse places to be. The Major was back in his seat with his clock when I paid attention to Mr Dunae speaking again.

'I have a last announcement to make. My wife and I have been recalled suddenly to our original home in Seattle on family matters.' The room went quiet again. 'I'm sure you'll all understand that these things must be attended to at times.'

Murmurings of understanding rose. 'As you know, Footner runs itself now anyway, and there's very little need for me here. So until we come back, possibly in a month, possibly a little more, my very capable assistant Mr Jack Butler is in charge of maintenance.' It was the first I had heard of it. I had no idea what Charles Dunae did from day to day. He would have done better to have appointed Wang Chi, Matthew, Simon, James or John the waiter. Mrs Underhill was looking up at Charles Dunae. Her smile had hardened, and she was not making understanding murmurs.

CHAPTER FOUR

HARRY WAS SITTING ON HIS TIN TRUNK, trying to tug the capote over his head, Edward watching him from his bunk. The capote stuck, and Harry sat there, resting, resting, before struggling again, and getting it down over himself. He rose, and made it as far as the door. There he stopped and leant against the wall, already too tired to pick up the rifle. When he reached down Edward called to him.

'Leave it until tomorrow, Harry. I'll find more fox and hare and wolverine bones by then. Meat, too, I'm sure. And I'll go hunting.'

'You wouldn't know what to look for,' said Harry. The words came slowly. 'What would you look for on a day like this? He was looking upward as he spoke, his eyes running over the ceiling, as if he was outside already and there might be duck there, or one of the swans, high and impossible to shoot. 'Ptarmigan,' he said. 'Ptarmigan. This would be a day for ptarmigan.'

'Right, Harry. It would be ptarmigan,' said Edward. He stood up. 'Of course it would be ptarmigan. I'll get one. A brace, maybe. *Non recuso laborem.*'

'No,' said Harry. His head had sunk on his chest, then rose with a snap, his attempt at looking alert on again. He had the rifle in his hand now. He opened the door and went out, almost upright, leaving the door open behind him. I could see Edward looking at the door, willing himself to rise and close it. I got up and limped across and pulled it shut and fell back onto the bunk.

Hours, so long later, darkness already falling, I was breaking up wood, Edward at the table making a candle from fox grease. There was a scrabbling outside. Edward heard it too.

He rose from the chair, and walked slowly and stooped to the door. For those seconds before he opened it I thought, 'Oh, the caribou are here. I'll get the rifle and we'll get a caribou.' Then I knew it wasn't. It would be Harry, and he would have ptarmigan or a hare or a wolverine. And then Edward tugged the door open and Harry was on his hands and knees outside, and I knew how deluded I had been. No miracle had happened. No bird had sat until Harry's quivering legs had taken him close to it, until his wavering hands had raised the .303 and steadied and put a bullet into it. He had refused to bring a shotgun. The rage was rising in me. I wanted to slap him and slap him, take his head and beat it on the frozen earth floor until the blood ran. I went over it again like I had a thousand times by now: this hateful, snobbish, dangerous fool.

Edward had his hands under Harry's arms and got him to his feet. Harry pointed back out into the snow. He mumbled something. Then again. 'The rifle.' I took the crutch and went past them and outside into the dying light. I walked about a hundred yards, following the tracks where Harry had crawled towards the cabin, and there was the old Lee-Enfield where he had dropped it. I picked it up and trailed it after me. There wasn't one of us with the strength left to raise and aim it, but it was ours and I was taking it.

In the morning Harry, red eyed, so sunken-faced, said he felt better, and that we must all go hunting. He doled out thickly sugared tea, 'to charge us up', and we left early for once, at about nine o'clock, Edward and I wrapped in blankets, Harry again wearing the one capote. I had the second rifle. By about a hundred yards it was clear I was limping so badly I was holding them up.

'We'll fan out,' said Harry. 'There's no point in us staying together. You go there, Jack. Where it's flatter.' Everywhere was flat. He was pointing along the river. 'We'll go north.' He set off again with Edward, him as empty-handed as every other day. I went forward slowly for about two hours, seeing nothing to shoot. But then I wasn't going to surprise any animals, lumbering along and trailing my foot, trailing the crutch. The wind was rising and the dry snow froze on my face even under the blanket. I turned back towards the cabin. When I got there Harry was already in his bunk. There was no sign of Edward.

'I'm all in,' said Harry. 'Played out.' I wanted to collapse onto the wooden case, but instead I set and lit the stove. I made tea and gave him some, and he drank it and lay down again and said nothing more for a while. Then, 'In Edmonton. You saw Miss Hughes?' He waited.

'Yes.' A pretty young woman.

'We were engaged for three years.' I let him wait again. 'I could have what Edward has. And some day you'll marry too.' Whatever I thought at that moment I kept to myself. 'There was a place near Long View... ranching would have been a good life. I would have children. I wouldn't be here.'

'Would you like more tea?' His self-pity was worse than his bombast.

'But I went to the North with Critchell. One year away too many for Olwyn.'

There was silence, which I had no intention of filling. He lay on, eyes red-rimmed, the bones of his face jagged above the black beard, in the filth of his blankets. 'She's a good woman,' he said. Eventually he seemed to sleep.

WEDNESDAY, 15TH MAY 1918

I was riding along River Road from the Government Bridge back into Footner. It had been a gusty day with little clouds high-up, but like every other day here in the rainshadow of the Coast Mountains no rain had fallen. Maybe there would never be a day in Footner when I would look up and the sky would be clearing after rain.

Ahead of me a long, slow-moving freight train curved away towards town. I came closer and still the great train ran. I kept pace with the last carriages clanking and rattling beside me, and then it pulled ahead slowly, and by the time I got to Footner it had stopped in the long siding.

The driver climbed down, and the fireman, and walked off towards the CPR cabin. I rode along the side away from the little platform, looking at the wagons. There were cattle trucks, dozen after dozen of them. Flat cars for timber. I peered through the cracks and vents of the closed wagons. There were some with straw still littering the floor, and balls of horse dung. All were empty. I dropped the lines and dismounted and climbed up and tried the door of a wagon. It had no lock and the door slid open readily. It was clean-looking, with a heap of straw at the other end.

Here, far from the cities and towns, no one was bothering about locking up wagons. There was no bull to club off a rider. Anybody could step aboard a train like this. You could take food and water and make up a bed in the straw, and be comfortable all the way to the west. Step off outside Vancouver. Then a slow walk into the rest of your life. Anybody could do that. A woman. A woman with a child.

'Have you lost something?' I spun round. A railway worker in a dark blue suit stood on the gravel below me. He wasn't carrying a stick or a big spanner. 'We've even got trains with seats in them if you were thinking of going somewhere.' It was one of those voices that are half of their old country and something else vague and uncertain and not quite that of the new.

'I'm just looking.' I jumped down, landing on purpose close to him, I suppose to show I had nothing to hide, and wasn't afraid.

'You haven't got tired of working for Mrs Underhill and the BCHEC already, have you?' He was in his mid thirties, red haired under the railroad cap, a moustache to match. 'You have to try really hard here not to know everybody and what they're doing.'

'You're a long way from home.'

'From Savona? Naw, that's not far.' He had a mobile face, of the kind that would make all he said seem intended to be funny, whether it was or not.

'You're from Ireland.'

He nodded once. 'A long, long time ago. From little Listowel. As best I remember.'

'I'm from Omagh.' It might be useful to know an Irishman at the rail station. 'Not that long ago.'

'I'd heard it was Armagh. But I'm a Canadian now, however I sound. Kerry will never see me again. So. How can I help you?' There had been a change of tone, something brisk in the last words.

'I was looking at the train and thinking ahead to when the apples will be shipped out. Gathering information.'

He stood another moment and then began to walk away.

'Come on over and have a mug of tea,' he said. I led the horse over the gravel beside him. 'To meet a stranger in Footner these days is not that common, Mr Butler. I'm Terry Sullivan. The supposed head man of the CPR here.' He twisted round and held out his hand. I shook it.

'Yes. Jack Butler.'

'How did they get you roped in anyway?'

'I needed a job.'

'Fair enough. And now you're the head man of the BCHEC.'

'Supposed. Mr Dunae's house and office are locked. There's nothing I can do.' I'd been saying to anybody I came across that I wasn't responsible for anything. I tied up the cayuse, and followed him to the wooden cabin. Another CPR worker, plumper, older, sat on the bench outside, smoking a cigarette and with a newspaper on his knee. From inside came the rattle of plates and voices chattering and the smell of bacon frying.

'Are they still beating the tar out of each other over there?' asked Terry of the CPR man with the paper.

'They're taking a day off at the minute,' said the second CPR man. 'But did you hear the Red Baron was shot down, the scum, and by a Canadian, too?'

'This is our visitor, Mr Jack Butler,' said Terry. 'Have you left any tea?'

'There's a bit. A strong bit, eh. The way you like it.' He was Canadian.

'I'm sure,' said Terry. He went into the cabin. I sat down with the other CPR man.

'Albert,' he said. 'It's a fine evening.' He put the cigarette into his mouth and held out his hand. I shook it. All this English handshaking. 'Are you following the War then?' The cigarette danced about.

'On and off.'

'How are you liking Footner?'

I nodded, as if I was thinking. 'It seems a fine place to work for a while.'

'It's looking good at the moment. The blossom out.'

'Yes.'

'It won't last a week. Too dry, and the winds. Will you be settling?'

'I'm not a settling man. I move on.'

'Even most of the people of Footner have moved on.' It was Terry, back with two enamel mugs. He put one in my hand. The tea looked very pale, with small white spots of gone-off milk on top. 'It was a bit strong so I put plenty of milk in it. And who can blame them?' His head was shaking. 'It's one of those things.'

I nodded. 'It's one of those things.'

'Footner,' he said. He sipped at his tea, lowered the tin mug and began to lift spots of milk off with an oil-stained forefinger.

'What was here before?'

'A junction where the rails met.' He put the mug on the ground and began to fill a long briar pipe. 'Old Pennie, who owned all this place when I first came, over-wintered cattle on it. But he had a couple of apple trees in a hollow, down by the Jimmie.' He pointed with the stem of the pipe. 'For his own use. The poor things were hardly alive even at that. Ferocious summers and winters here. Then some genius, seeing his trees, decided the whole area was another Okanagan. Do you know how much was paid for this?' His head went up to indicate the land around us. 'Two hundred and thirty thousand dollars.' He grimaced, and then smiled again.

Albert was snorting beside me.

'Old Pennie's away on the west coast now, still laughing his head off.'

I gave a short laugh. 'The mad English people. They have ways of their own.' I was showing them they could talk as they liked in front of me.

'If only they had asked somebody from Ashcroft or Cache Creek or Savona,' Albert said. 'But no.' He drew on his cigarette for a bit.

'I'm sure. So what was it like when they were all here? Before the War?'

'A laugh a minute,' said Albert. 'We'd sit here in the evenings and watch them go about. It's nothing now like it used to be. Very quiet now.'

'They had great sports days. I'll say that for them,' said Terry. He had his pipe going well and drew on it. 'About two or three every week, it seemed like sometimes.'

'More sports days than work days,' said Albert.

'Ah, we'll be putting Jack off his new employers,' said Terry. 'But is there much there you didn't know already?'

I shook my head. 'Only the two hundred and thirty thousand dollars.' I sat on, drinking a little of the tea. 'The empty trains go through all the time then?'

'There's one most days, heading west. A lot of freight heads east, for the War and all. Not much freight west.'

'I can't keep Mrs Underhill waiting. My dinner will be ready.'

'That's a lovely arrangement you have there.'

I was sorry I had spoken of Mrs Underhill. I got to my feet. 'Thank you for the mug of whatever it was.'

'Any time,' said Terry. 'Come back any time for a chin wag.'

'Sure.'

All the way home I was thinking of old Pennie, away in the west, the other side of the Coast Mountains, where the rains fell, where the land was lush and rich, where crops of all sorts grew, and where the summers and winters weren't ferocious.

Monday, 20th May 1918, Victoria Day.

We stood beside a democrat at Twin Lakes, a mile or more up in the hills behind Footner. The ground here was too steep and rocky for even the orchardists of Footner to attempt cultivation. But there were aspen and birch trees for shade, and some grass to lie and run on, and two shallow ponds.

'Oh, it's so sad,' said Susan Fellowes. 'When I visited before the War…'

'Before the War,' said Mrs Underhill. 'Sssh.' She put her finger to her lips. 'No bad words. Hector can't remember before the War. Can you, Hector? And he's perfectly happy.'

'But I can,' said Susan. 'When this site was thronged, and the Recreation Grounds in town were thronged, and the Hotel in the evening would be filled with dancers. When the sprung floor was used for other things than storing apples. When Victoria Day was an *event*.'

'It's an event now,' said Mrs Underhill. Like her friend she was dressed in a white blouse and skirt and narrow dark tie. 'We are here. Everybody has a holiday. The children will play.'

'All the few who haven't been carried off to Blighty. Miss Ricketts' one class.'

Under the seats of the Fellowes' democrat, and no doubt the other wagons, were hampers with chicken and sandwiches and cakes and fruit and bottled drinks. Croquet hoops and mallets. Bats, and balls for throwing, and balls for hitting, and balls for kicking. Tapes for measuring jumps and throws, for the dozen elderly men and forty or so ladies of Footner, and the eight or nine children.

A half dozen of the ladies, and Jameson, the young man with a limp, were spreading rugs and setting up chairs and folding tables in the shade of the trees. Old Willie Woolley and a young man I hadn't seen before, a sleeve of his jacket empty, hung bunting among the aspens and birches. Dogs raced and barked. Mrs Fortesque, with a black armband, and Miss Myers, her sister, neighbours of Mrs Fellowes, walked slowly past, linked arm in arm, towards the marshy shore of the nearest pond.

'My father-in-law got Willie to drive the Myers, Midge Andrews, Billy Fiske and Major Sidgwick up this morning,' said Susan.

The bunting blew away from the thin branches and fell among the grass and boulders. On the most level piece of ground boys and old men were setting up cricket stumps and swinging arms in practice bowling.

'Look at that,' said Susan. She pointed at the cricketers, smiling. 'Do you remember Reggie belting the ball into the water, time after time, and not being allowed to play any more?'

'Yes.' Mrs Underhill nodded.

'He said he couldn't help it,' said Susan. 'That he only had the one stroke. My giddy young future husband.' She looked away from the cricketers, and at the ponds. 'And Edward,' she said. 'Your Edward trying to make his horse swim in the far lake, and the water only coming up to its knees?'

'I don't remember that. Let's walk. Come on, Hector.'

'And the children complaining because he had muddied the water so for their boats?'

'No. Not Edward.'

I let them walk ahead of me. A boy was holding Major Sidgwick's arm and leading him to a higher place beyond the cricket area where the bare trunk of a lodge pole pine had been erected. In the boy's other hand was a folded flag.

'The Major's still taking charge of proceedings,' said Susan. 'I'm pleased to see that.'

'Of course he is,' said Mrs Underhill. 'It *is* Victoria Day.'

We had stopped walking, and watched the boy guide the old man's hands to the rope.

'Like last year. And the one before,' said Susan.

'Some things persist,' said Mrs Underhill. The flag tied on at last, it was hauled up the pole by both old man and boy.

'Not a lot of ceremony,' said Susan.

'Our musicians are not around,' said Mrs Underhill. 'Except of course Miss Ricketts.'

'And Fanny couldn't get the piano up here.' Both women laughed and moved on. 'And you didn't try?'

Mrs Underhill shook her head.

'Poor Miss Ricketts,' said Susan. 'The only woman to come to Footner and not get a husband. Well, it's true. Even I got one.'

'Maybe Miss Ricketts doesn't want one.' After a dozen steps she turned to me. 'Our laconic Jack. What are you going to do today? Are you a cricketer?'

'No.'

'Footballer?'

I shook my head.

'Perhaps you'll join the children in the egg and spoon?'

'Maybe.'

'Laconic but not inscrutable Jack,' said Susan Fellowes. Her finger pointed at me. 'A little smile.'

'Supervise them in the sack race?' said Mrs Underhill.

'If duty so calls me.' I had no intention of doing any of this. 'I'll unload and load the democrat, and drive it back down that terrible trail. I'll enjoy what is my day off as well.'

'I don't think you'll get away with that,' said Susan.

'Oh no. As the most able male here you will be involved, want it or not.' Mrs Underhill turned away. 'Miss Ricketts,' she called suddenly. Small Miss Ricketts, her light brown hair beginning to grey, looked up. 'We have a volunteer here for setting a manly example in the egg and spoon race. And many, many other events.'

'Mrs Underhill…'

'Do not hesitate to call on him.'

'He is champing at the bit, Miss Ricketts,' said Susan Fellowes. 'Only shyness is holding him back. Really he will be happy to do heaps.'

'Thank you, Mr Butler. It will be much appreciated,' said Miss Ricketts.

'I shall be back shortly Miss Ricketts.' I kept walking. 'Thank you, Mrs Underhill. And Mrs Fellowes.'

'So you'd better not hit the Pale Ale too heavily,' said Susan Fellowes as I hurried on.

'One or two have before,' said Mrs Underhill.

'There used to be quite a lot of that, actually,' said Susan. 'I remember Captain Carlyon turning a nice cart right over on the way down. Not a wheel left on it, and his arm broken.'

'What laughs.'

'And the three-legged races the men used to do,' said Susan. She was looking up at the hills. 'I remember it.' She put her hands in the pockets of her skirt. 'The Chetwynds. The Lloyds. Those Weirs. So many.' I heard her take a deep breath. 'And Frank,' she said. 'Little Frankie Groome.' We walked on for another dozen steps.

'Yes,' said Mrs Underhill. 'Frankie Groome.'

The late morning sun was already hot. Mr Fellowes, Midge Andrews with his empty sleeve, and Billy Fiske, crutches beside him, sheltered together under an Indian parasol. Dogs waded for coolness in the pond near where Mrs Fortesque walked with her sister. Hector ran to join them, entered the water, came out immediately and shook himself on Miss Myers.

'They…' said Susan.

We watched Miss Myers wave him away.

'Do you think they remember such things?' said Susan. 'Now?' For a moment I thought she meant the dogs. 'Wherever they are,' said Susan. 'Do you think they remember such things? How days like this used to be? How they used to be?'

Mrs Underhill continued to watch the pond. 'I wonder what events we shall help with today?'

'Sarah…' Susan turned to her.

Mrs Underhill put her hand on her friend's arm.

'We shall keep on as we are,' she said. 'Isn't this a marvellous day?'

They walked on another few steps, Mrs Underhill still holding the arm. Eventually Susan Fellowes nodded.

'Anyway,' she said. She sniffed. 'Anyway. There's young Collingwood and the youngest Durant girl playing hide and seek amongst the birches. Yes. Some things are as they were. As they should be.' She looked around her. She smiled. 'But have you noticed? There are more dogs here than children. Why didn't we think ahead enough to organise some dog events?'

'Races. Agility. Swimming.'

'Wouldn't that be a laugh?'

'Absolutely.' Mrs Underhill linked her friend's arm.

'A dogs' six-legged race,' said Susan.

'The dogs' egg and spoon.'

'Yes. The dogs have to eat the egg and bury the spoon.'

They laughed again, and walked on and I followed. I was content to be with them, content to feel largely forgotten.

How long each day seemed then. A day like this Victoria Day picnic. Or any working day, on the flume, or fencing, or weeding, or at Sarah's place. The evening meal, sitting on the porch, talking quietly. An idle Sunday afternoon, walking with her and the dog. As if we moved slowly, spoke slowly, time hanging overhead, unchanging, awaiting our call to serve us. As if.

The air was cooling, the sun falling towards the dark hills. The children tired and quiet and staying close to their mothers. Major Sidgwick and Mr Fellowes and other old men sat in circled chairs and smoked and talked and dozed. A couple of women moved, unspeaking, among the picnic things, carrying a bottle or a glass or a plate. The wagons stood empty, the horses waiting, the shadows long. It was time to go back to town, past time, but no one had packed up the rugs or the other picnic things, nor drawn the stumps yet.

'I observed you quelling dissension in the egg and spoon race today, Jack,' said Mrs Underhill. 'And with an iron hand.'

The three of us and Hector were on the little height overlooking the cricket area. A wicker picnic hamper, well ransacked during the afternoon, and now tidied up and the straps buckled, sat nearby.

'And how you took command of the sack race and throwing the bean bag,' said Susan. 'I was impressed.'

The two women lay side by side, resting on their forearms on the grass. I sat with my back to the lodge pole pine, Hector asleep in the dust beside me. Above us the Union Flag hung quietly.

'You showed a commendable air of authority generally,' said Mrs Underhill. 'I heard Miss Ricketts praise you for it.'

'Very military,' said Susan.

'I also ate many sandwiches and cake and drank many bottles of ginger beer.'

'You said you wouldn't play cricket, though, Jack,' said Mrs Underhill.

'But you played cricket, Jack,' said Susan. Her eyes widened, as if in astonishment.

'I ran after the ball. I didn't bowl nor bat. I would not necessarily want to field, as they call it, again.'

'You put up hurdles, and demonstrated how to jump them,' said Mrs Underhill. 'And how to fall over them. You put up this flag again when it fell down, and didn't tell Major Sidgwick.'

'The games finished with the children climbing on you,' said Susan.

'Let's not make his head any bigger,' said Mrs Underhill. 'But you were surprisingly amiable. For a grumpus.'

'Is that how you see me?'

I watched them, these two women, side by side in their white dresses, quiet again, both intelligent, both attractive. Both born into a privilege I would not know. That most in Canada, in England, would not know. Or maybe just a sense of privilege. They had husbands, also privileged, or thinking they were. The air around them seemed very calm, so calm it was almost tangible. I put my hand out, and opened my fingers, and closed them again. I could hold it. Almost hold it, this moment, this quiet, peaceful day.

Beyond my hand was the edge of the smaller pond, the beginning of the trees. A dark bird darted from the trees, circled and swooped over the cricket area, unseen by the men and boys. Then another. Not birds, but the first bats, hunting. Susan Fellowes plucked a blade of grass and put it in her mouth. She too was watching the bats. She took the grass out again.

'Miss Weir will have been busy getting the Hotel decorated. Miss Ricketts and the band will play My Chocolate Soldier Sammy Boy. We at least can still gather there.'

'Hmm,' said Mrs Underhill.

'How does Eleanor bear up like that?' Susan Fellowes shook her head. 'Anyway. There might be a few fireworks from the CPR chaps. Mr Dunae didn't leave any money for a display, did he, Jack?'

'I have no authority to spend ten cents. I don't know if there is ten cents.' I watched them. 'I asked Willie why there were no CPR men here. He said the CPR men never wanted to come.' I hadn't even asked about the Chinese. 'Willie is very loyal to Footner.'

'Willie's lived all over Canada,' said Susan. 'And now he's over sixty he wants to end his days among his own kind. That's how he has put it.'

'No manager's speech this year in praise of the British Empire,' said Mrs Underhill. 'Because no manager. Unless you want to do it, Jack?'

Susan Fellowes leant closer to her. 'Is he ever coming back?'

There was silence for a while. I put my finger down to the bare earth. A pale brown mottled moth was struggling through the dust. It stopped, fluttered, and went still. I didn't think Charles Dunae was ever coming back either. As long as my wages were paid into the bank in Ashcroft every month I didn't care. The manager was an empty cypher. These women's husbands were empty cyphers. What else could they be? The memory of a batsman with one swing, abandoned cricket pads, a lifeless image in a photograph? What part had they in this Victoria Day, in Footner, now?

'And Hector has loved it, I know,' said Mrs Underhill. She twisted round to see the dog and smiled at me and looked away again. 'Lots of picnic food to clear up and other dogs to play with, and swims in the lakes. He's exhausted.'

'They say dogs are happy because they live for the moment,' said Susan. 'No bothers about the past or the future. So I've read somewhere.'

'How wise then is my Hector,' said Mrs Underhill.

'But we are not dogs,' said Susan. She chewed on the end of her piece of grass. 'It was Gordon Weir who rode his horse into the lake.' She lay looking towards the bats and cricket area for a little longer. 'After the War...' She turned suddenly towards Mrs Underhill. 'After the War... is that not the way we should be thinking? Looking ahead?' Mrs Underhill rolled over on the grass, closer to her friend, looking up into her face. 'After the War,' said Susan. 'My husband back here. Your husband back.' Sarah Underhill watched her friend. 'All the men back. Some of the men. The place packed with other young women and young chaps once more. Brothers' friends and friends of friends. Just like before. Is that what you think?'

'After the War. Yes.'

'It's this day,' said Susan. 'The holiday. A day that back then, like so many days before the War, was always such a jolly time. That was all we seemed to have then. Jolly days. Jollier evenings.'

'This was a wonderful day,' said Mrs Underhill. 'It was a very good day.'

'But those jolly times,' said Susan. She was looking, not down at Mrs Underhill, but across the grass and over the picnic area. Nothing was happening except two dogs still splashing in the nearer pond. 'Are gone for ever.'

'I am happy,' said Mrs Underhill. I watched the moth in the bare dust. It was not still, for its wings just perceptibly vibrated. I put a finger under it and picked it up and moved it into a tussock of bunch grass. I thought I should say something, wise or not.

'This has been a very pleasant day.' It was true.

Susan Fellowes shook her head, as if waking up. 'And what am I doing here? I should be nursing.'

'Susan…'

'What are any of us doing here? I should be in France.' Her voice rose. 'Somewhere. But not here.'

'You are doing what I am doing.' Mrs Underhill took her friend's hand and held it. 'What other sisters and wives and mothers are doing. What we should be doing. Keeping the homes and land going for the men to come back to.'

'Do you believe that? Do you?' Susan looked down now at Mrs Underhill. She leant a little closer again, and quietly now, so I could just barely hear the words, as if it were a secret, she said, 'Because I'm not sure I do.'

'Yes.' Mrs Underhill was definite. 'I do.'

'Sarah…' Susan spoke quietly again. 'I'm not sure I ever did.'

'Well. I do.'

'Our lives are slipping away, our men are dying, and we are doing nothing of worth.'

Mrs Underhill squeezed the hand she held, and shook it for emphasis, and let it go. 'Believe me.'

The younger woman raised herself once more on her elbows. She nodded towards where Mrs Fortesque and her sister sat, apart from the others, beneath one of the taller birches.

'Is Johnny Fortesque coming back? Mary Fortesque is leaving in a month. Her sister with her. The house and property will lie empty and unsold. Like others have.' She gestured towards the one-armed young man tramping through the grass and picking up the bunting. 'Is Midge Andrews' arm coming back? How much longer will he be here? And Billy Fiske, won't he have more of a future somewhere else?'

'Then some new people shall get bargains after the War.' Mrs Underhill spoke firmly. 'Bargains. That's all I can say.' She rolled over and away from Susan Fellowes and got to her feet. 'Reggie will be back, and Edward will be back. Life will resume.' She brushed down her dress, and stood looking at the people below. 'Now. Let's get on with it. Major Sidgwick—' she called. 'Major Sidgwick. I beg your pardon for disturbing you.' Across the cricket area Mr Fellowes nudged the even older man in the arm, and the Major jerked awake. 'Shall we get underway? Get back to town before dark? The bats are out, hunting moths for their suppers.'

The old man was getting to his feet. 'What?' he said. He was peering around as if he could still see. 'What's that, old boy?'

I got to my feet, and picked up the wicker picnic hamper and carried it away in the direction of the democrat.

CHAPTER FIVE

I<small>T WAS LATE WHEN</small> E<small>DWARD CAME BACK</small>. His mouth was open, and he was panting.

'I saw twenty caribou,' he said. 'But far away. I followed, and when I thought I had lost them I got one in deep snow. But I had forgotten to take the knife from you, Harry, and it was dark by then. But we'll all eat tomorrow, if the wolves don't get it.'

Harry's blackened and chewed lips moved, and his tongue came out. It was close to a grin. He was himself again. But we could do nothing that night. I lay awake, thinking of the carcass in the snow, of the wolves, glad for once the wind never stopped twisting and changing and hammering around the cabin walls. In the morning we followed Edward and to my surprise we found the caribou. In the wind and drifting snow wolves hadn't got it. We cut it up and carried all we could back to the cabin, beating into that ceaseless hard wind. By then Harry was again hardly able to move and collapsed onto his bunk. My foot was hurting so much I couldn't move either. It hurt all the more as our bodies thawed out around the stove, the smells driving us crazy as we waited while Edward fried slabs of meat.

For the next four days the wind howled and snow fell and we ate the meat and no one went out. Once I unwrapped my foot and looked at where the axe had slashed it. It looked the same as the day I had done it, the flesh white, the cut deep and gaping. I wrapped the same strips of dirty bloody cloth, all there was, around it again.

By the time the storm blew itself out there were only the bones and sinews of the caribou left. The next day we all went out to hunt as we were able, and all came back with nothing. On March 6th Harry said he was going to go as far as the trapline, but came back soon after, empty-handed. That night he began to talk of caribou again.

'We know there are caribou,' he said. 'There's always caribou. But for some reason they're not on their usual path. They'll most likely be farther north. We should take sugar in our pockets and go north. We should follow the caribou.'

'You don't know the caribou are there, Harry,' I said.

'Where else are they? They're not here.'

'That's… We can't stalk a caribou herd. We can't walk long distances. I can't walk like that.'

'No. You'll stay here, on their old crossing place, like you did before. It will be Edward and myself on the trail.'

'Look…Edward doesn't have a gun…' Why wasn't Edward arguing this? 'Why do you take him out day after day?' Harry sucked and gummed away on a bit of caribou bone. 'Using up what strength he has. Why don't we have three guns? Why don't we have a shotgun?' Harry threw down the bone, picked up another, sucked it, and didn't look back at me. There was no out-reasoning Harry if he wouldn't converse with you.

It was March 9th before they left, for Harry kept resting. All our scraps were long gone by then. They each had a pot of sugar and this time they took the tent with them. I had the flour and the rest of the sugar.

They were gone about two hours when at last I shot something. I'd gone out, walking in short bursts, putting down the crutch and waiting quietly every now and again. Then I saw a fox trailing its hindquarters, probably injured escaping from one of our own faraway traps. I shot it, took it back, and over the day ate all of it, and boiled the bones and kept the water to drink. Later I took the fur out and buried it in the snow.

On the night of March 11th Harry was fumbling again at the door. He had left Edward in the tent and walked back along the frozen river for more ammunition and a spare pair of snowshoes. He said little, except that they had got nothing yet, 'but soon would. It felt right'. He rested until just before first light, and then fried a little of the flour into a pancake, and filled it with sugar.

'Edward's in a good position there,' he said, talkative now he had rested. 'He's set fair. By the time I get back he should have some animals. Caribou, certainly. Half a dozen, maybe, for he's coming on as a shot. We haven't seen the tracks, but then the snow is always drifting. They will be there, for a certainty. Or soon.'

Then he was gone again, carrying the ammunition and snowshoes, things he could have taken with him in the first place, all the way once more to the tent where Edward waited. With his supposed slain half dozen caribou.

I stayed where I was, crying out for food, for warmth, trying to balance up saving energy with going out for wood and the vain hope of killing something.

SUNDAY, 9TH JUNE 1918

'The sun is like honey,' she said. 'Golden rich honey.'

The heat was intense on my bare forearms. On the top of my head and on the back of my neck. My shoulders under the cotton of the shirt felt as if they were close to a roaring fire. But there was no roaring fire, and the only sound was that of the Thompson. The loving lap of the Thompson. Close to shore on the wide bend all was calm, but ten, twelve feet out the water tore past. A stick would go by, flying, turning, dipping out of sight, to rise again forty feet away, and spin on towards Lytton and the great Fraser and through the Coast Mountains to Vancouver and the far Pacific.

On the gritty sand of the bank the three of us sat in a row: Hector, Mrs Underhill, myself. On a rug in front of us lay the remains of a picnic: plates, cutlery, glasses, bread, cheese, chicken pie, apple pie, a ginger beer bottle, the things we had carried down from the horses.

Her feet were bare. Her small pale feet. She took off her hat, turned her face upwards.

'I can feel the weight of it. The weight of the sun.' Her head turned from side to side. 'However.' She lowered her face again, put on the wide straw hat. 'The complexion, do you know.' Then she tossed back her head again anyway. 'But I love the weight of the sun on my face.' Then she looked at me quickly, and laughed, and the dimple came in her cheek, and we sat quietly.

Little flies were dancing across the water in the sunlight, swirling, rising, falling.

'Summer days in England. In Wheathampstead. Tell me about them.'

'Tell me, tell me, tell me,' she said. 'No. You tell me. Tell me instead about summer days in Ireland. Did it rain much?'

I sat there saying nothing, feeling the sun, watching the flies like motes. How far away was Ireland. How far away all the past. The past of a night of rain, the day warming up into sunlight after. Not far enough away. Not yet. Here there was no sound but the running and lapping of water. She had not pursued it.

Instead I watched her rise, and, holding up her dress, wade to her ankles in the Thompson, the dog splashing around her. How the sparkle of the water hurt the eyes. She stood there, her face turned upwards, eyes closed, shimmering in white. Hector had gone further into the river.

'Hector.' The dog kept splashing around. 'No, Hector. Come back.' She dropped her dress, the skirts falling in the water, and bent and picked up a stick from the eddies beside her and waved it at the dog. The dog kept on wading out and then suddenly the current had picked him up and he was not wading but drifting rapidly downriver. He turned, paddling, paddling harder. 'Hector!' A wild call. I got to my feet. The dog was thrashing at the water, going faster away from us. 'Hector!' The dog turned again, got his feet to the bottom. He stood there, twenty or thirty yards downriver, up to his belly. He lapped at the water. 'Hector!' The dog looked up, went back to drinking. She waded out, the water tearing at the bottom of her dress, grasped his collar and pulled him towards the shore. She stood there panting, holding him tight by the collar. She swallowed. 'Fast and clear and beautiful Thompson. But we can't come back here, Hector. No more.'

I sat down again and stayed there in the burning sun and smelt the young sage and the juniper and watched them: her wet dress, and her bare feet on the stones, and her watching the Thompson.

SATURDAY, 29TH JUNE 1918

About three o'clock. The sun baking the ground and the air and everything in it. All silent and still. I had started work in one of the farther reaches of the Underhill place, digging sage out of the irrigation ditches. Happy, alone, I did what I seldom did, for I haven't much of the music: I sang out into the heavy, unmoving air… *In Kilkenny it is reported, on marble stone there, as black as ink…*

When I turned she was coming up the last steps towards me, slowly but steadily, in her dark pencil skirt and white blouse and narrow tie. I stood there, the spade in my hand. She was flushed from the walk, panting a little, Hector trotting behind her.

'How are you, Jack?' I nodded. She stood for another moment, looking around the orchard, as if checking. 'Is everything all right?' I said nothing. She turned away towards the Thompson. There it was, the glint of sun and water, the bend, the land rising behind. All that water, so close to the orchards parched of it. But she hadn't walked up here in her pencil skirt to ask me if everything was all right.

'Tell me what it is.'

She looked back at me, her head angled to the side. I stuck the spade in the ground. She stood on for another moment.

'Susan Fellowes has gone,' she said. 'My one good friend. She left this morning, suddenly. She's going to stay with her sister in Montreal.'

'I'm sorry.'

'She intends to train as a nurse.' I squatted down and stroked Hector behind the ears. He panted in his thick wiry coat. 'Reggie's father will take care of the property on his own. He is active enough. Or else he won't, but she couldn't stay there another day. That's how she put it. And doesn't see why she should.' She turned to me, open-eyed, as if she might have to defend Susan Fellowes. 'I don't blame her. She was married for three months when Reggie enlisted. It's not like Edward and I. It's not like that.'

'No.'

'She says she'll be back for a visit, definitely, for Christmas. I don't think she will ever come back here.' A little silence fell between us. 'Of course I miss her. I shall miss her more in months to come.' I straightened again. 'But she is doing what she feels she must. Are you nearly finished here?' I hadn't long begun.

'I'm finished.'

'Walk down to the benches with me, then.'

She was so close beside me it seemed natural to hold out my arm to her, and she took it, and linked thus we went down over the uneven ground of the orchard towards the lower bench lands.

'I had a great craving today to talk...' She didn't finish her sentence. She had a craving to talk to Susan? Talk to her husband? 'Or just for some news,' she went on. 'Real news. One way or another. More than the newspapers say.' She looked ahead, towards the river. 'That's what I miss Susan for, to jolly me out of it.'

I couldn't think what to say either, to jolly her out of it.

'The sea is wide,' I said, saying what had been in my head anyway, 'and you cannot swim over.'

I thought her grip on my arm tightened then. Maybe I imagined it. We went on.

FRIDAY, 12TH JULY 1918

Ahead was supper and the warm quiet evening. Then the weekend on the farm. As I passed the Hotel there was Major Sidgwick in evening dress, leaning on his cane. Hearing someone approach he raised his hand.

'Good evening, Major.'

'Ah. Mr Butler.'

'The Twelfth of July, Major. At least the boys had a good day for it.'

'I beg your pardon?'

'Nothing, Major. An Irish thing.'

'Ah. Otherwise all serene?'

'All serene.'

'I hear we made ninety-seven degrees today. A proper scorcher. Don't have that in Ireland, eh?'

'It'll be hundred tomorrow, Major,' and I laughed, to please him, and end the conversation. As I rode on there was a whistle from the CPR station. I looked that way before I thought. Terry waving, calling me towards him. I turned the cayuse, dropped the lines, stepped up onto the platform, took the seat beside him.

'Another one of the same coming up tomorrow,' said Terry. High above us were still and broken wisps of cirrus. Sarah would be taking in the washing, hard from the sun. I nodded. He filled his pipe. 'You don't smoke then?'

I shook my head. And giving Hector his supper.

'You never did? There's a great solace in the tobacco.'

'I never got the habit.'

Several ladies, also in evening dress, now escorted by Major Sidgwick, or escorting him, made their way slowly into the Hotel. Albert came out of the cabin behind us, holding an enamel mug of tea.

'They're in a little world of their own,' he said, looking over at the women and the Major.

'I've come through Assiniboia, and Windermere, and places like that. There's other Footner's.'

'Cattle and apples,' said Terry. 'And money from home for the second sons and scallywags.'

'And dreamers. There were dreamers as well.'

'If there was a dream here...' said Terry, and he turned to me, and his mobile face became serious, '... it ended on August 4th 1914.'

'How happy they were,' said Albert. 'The War was going to be cricket and football and a big horse race all rolled into one.' He took a seat on the bench beside us. 'They didn't want to miss a minute of it.'

'A lot of people thought like that.' Why was I defending them?

'Did you?' said Terry. He was still watching me. Then he turned away and sipped his tea. 'What about you?'

'I might still join up.'

There was a pause, and then a quiet 'Oh,' from Terry. 'So you didn't want to join up in Ireland?'

'I was younger then, and footloose, and wanted to see the world.' It would be better to tell him something.

'I've two nephews in the War,' he said. 'There's a lot of Irishmen in the War.' I kept quiet. 'So when did you leave the oul home country then?'

'A long time ago and far far away.'

'Right,' he said. 'Right.' He drew on the pipe for a while. 'Right,' he said again. Albert drank his tea, and we all sat looking ahead, over at the Hotel. She was waiting.

'The Battle of Marne's going badly for those German bastards,' said Albert. 'The War's on the turn. So it says in the *Sentinel.*'

I stood up. 'It's time to go,' I said. 'It's time to get back.'

'You're a lucky, lucky man,' said Terry. 'Like that.'

I resented him saying it, that he was even thinking of Sarah, and I made no reply and mounted the cayuse and rode on.

MONDAY, 29TH JULY 1918

'Look,' she said.

She was a foot away on the porch, leaning back in a pine chair, pointing to a cloud, pink-rimmed with the low sun, in

77

the shape of a dog's head. A dog with its tongue out. I smiled. I turned, and she was watching me, seeing my reaction, still pointing. Then her hand was lowered, and she looked back at the cloud, smiling too.

The day was ending, a day of labour, of hot sun. The still air cooling.

There were the dark hills, and somewhere, below and out of sight, soundless, the Thompson.

The passing day.

Meanwhile the pink cloud moved on, so slowly, eastward. In a day, two, three days, whatever rain it held would pour out over the Shuswap or the Monashee or the Columbia or the far-away Rockies. It could fall as snow, become locked in a glacier. Maybe someday, many years from now, it would come past here again, flowing back towards the sea, quick and clear in our Thompson River. These fanciful things I was thinking as we sat together.

And when this water came past again, would I be here? Would it be our Thompson River? I could think right then, on that evening of the cooling air and the soft pink cloud in the shape of the dog's head, of nothing I wanted more than to still be coming back to this house at the end of the day, washing, eating a meal, sitting here on the porch with this woman, this sleeping dog, this cooling air, this content.

I was where I wanted to be. I wanted nothing to change. How clear, suddenly, that was. Would she know that?

'Everything is on hold,' she said. It was the way she spoke more than the words: I was understood, without speaking. I turned again to her, just a little so she might not see me watching. There was her cheek, her lips, her dark eyes looking ahead over the dark hills to the blue and grey metallic sky and the pink cloud.

'I used to be interested in so many things before the War,' she said. 'What was happening in art, in music, in politics, and especially with women's matters. There was so much, then. But I was never part of it. A spectator, waiting... for what I don't know. I should have been involved.'

Her hand came down to where Hector lay on the boards beside her. His head rose as if he knew the hand was descending, and her fingertips touched his head and fondled his thick hair. The dog's eyes remained closed and his head moved under her hand.

Here we were, her and I, and the cloud in the sky, both of us watching it.

SATURDAY, 17TH AUGUST 1918

I rested on the spade and looked up.

There was Mrs Underhill, in her working clothes of an old dress and boots, a scarf on her head, a hoe in her gloved hands, pulling, pulling at the dusty soil, working her way towards the far end of the orchard. I bent to my work again, digging around raspberry bushes between the trees. The earth, a fine dust in the wind and sun, was trickling back even as I dug. Some of the raspberry bushes were dead.

After a while I was at the corner, and I stepped through the young trees and the low dry bushes and across to the next ditch. It looked as if it had never received water from the small supply. Then I would make it deeper, and better, and more likely to get water. I thrust the spade into the falling earth. It was maybe an hour later when I heard her call from between the trees.

'Luncheon, Jack.'

I looked up through the sweat and dirt and there she was, Hector darting about ahead of her, coming from the direction of the house, holding a wicker basket by the handle. I flung down the spade. I flung myself down after it, in the little shade of one of the trees. The leaves were against my back, and brushed against my face at times like flies, but I was weary and hot and didn't move.

'It's not much,' she said. 'Bread, jam, cheese, tea.'

'You do know it would be cheaper if you paid me a dollar now and then and let me find my own bed and board?' She had turned back the wicker lid and was handing me a cheese sandwich.

'Then you would not be here as often,' she said, matter-of-factly. 'To do the things I need done. And other people would ask you to work for them, and offer you more money, and take you away from me.' She was putting out two cups and saucers. A tea pot was jammed into one corner of the basket. 'And there is cake. I have to make it tempting for you.' She was busy pouring tea. When she turned back again she was smiling. 'Am I not right?'

'I suppose so.'

'Yes, I am,' she said. 'It suits both of us.'

'When the War is over, when it doesn't suit any more, I'll be told to leave.' Slowly she took the lid from the tea pot and looked inside, and as slowly replaced it.

'You think that's the way it will be?' she said quietly. 'I thought you knew better.'

'Is that not what the town believes? That all will be well again, one of these fine days, and no more outsiders needed?'

She reached out and plucked a dead leaf from a raspberry bush. 'We should never have set these,' she said. 'There is little enough water and good soil for the trees.' She crumpled up the leaf into dust and turned her hand over and let the dust fall. 'One of these fine days… It's four years now. And the fine day is still not here.' She was looking at the ground where the crumpled leaf had fallen. 'Bob Hudson was the first, at Neuve Chapelle in March 1915. He was here, wandering about his orchard, standing in the Hotel trying to get a cricket team together, and then he was overseas, and then he was dead. Like that.' And she clicked her fingers. 'When Edward went away...' She swallowed, and thought. 'Then George Hamilton-Warde. Good old George, wild rider and coyote huntsman, of the Hotel bar and later the Seventh Battalion. Bought it, as they say, at the Second Battle of Ypres, April 1915. Then Johnny Fortesque and Eddie Durant, on the same day. How's that? Out, innings over, on July 1st 1916. The Somme. Then little Frankie Groome, on whom Susan was sweet, even after she married Reggie. She made no secret of it. Well, not to us. Frankie became...' Her voice fell for a moment. '...he became whatever he became on April 9th 1917 at Vimy Ridge. How we celebrated the Battle of Vimy Ridge. We all did. I too. The making of Canada, they say. And there is Gordon Weir of course. There is always Gordon. Our hero, not that they are not all heroes, at Moreuil Wood on March 31st 1918. Not long before you got here.' She sat on, looking ahead now into the warm distance. 'We have got off comparatively lightly, I expect. Some think so a little less than others.'

'Midge Andrews?' I gave Hector the last piece of my cheese sandwich.

'Arm taken off by shrapnel from a bombardment. Billy Fiske, his leg by machine gun fire. There's plenty of others, wounded, and patched up and returned to the Front, or they stay with their families in England, and will never come back here again. And it's not over. Who knows of whom we shall hear next.' She would have to be, must be, thinking of Edward.

'And Jameson? Of the bad leg.'

'Jameson. That was with the Footner Company of the 31st British Columbia Horse.'

'A cavalry charge, then.' I could see him, a young man, wild, on a horse in a world of barbed wire and machine guns and trenches.

'In a way. Not in France though.' She shook her head. Those heavy-lidded eyes closed for a moment, opened again. 'In Vernon, the last summer before the War. A good summer of course, as they all say it was, as if there is any other kind here. He was in Vernon for training. How they loved their training. Edward wasn't part of the militia, but about forty other chaps were. Shooting competitions and steeplechases. Lots of work on horseback. So useful in modern warfare. And the Victoria Cross Race. Has anyone told you of that?' I shook my head. 'Riflemen stood behind barricades and fired up the field, and a cannon would be let off, and chaps rode forward to retrieve their wounded comrade from under the very guns.' She was speaking quickly, a story so familiar to her. 'The wounded comrade was an old sack stuffed with straw, and the rounds were blanks of course. Mind you, the horses didn't know that. Ralph Chetwynd and Gordon Weir won prizes year after year. Highly commended and lots of mentions in the *Ashcroft Journal*.'

'Jameson fell off?'

'Do you know what Gordon Weir won his Victoria Cross for in France?' the quick speech went on. 'His real one? In Lord Strathcona's Horse, galloping forward in the face of the enemy, into machine guns. But this time the rounds weren't blanks. Nevertheless he did as well as usual. A triumphant cavalry charge, newspapers called it. Over seventy percent of the men wounded or killed. No mention of the horses.' Now she stopped. After a while she spoke again. 'Yes. Jameson. He hadn't even entered the Victoria Cross Race. It was during the celebrations later. Ralph Chetwynd and Gordon Weir were racing stolen hay wagons—I beg their pardon: hay wagons borrowed from friends who hadn't yet been asked—down Mission Street, and Gordon Weir knocked Jameson down and ran two wheels over him. Crippled him. Poor Jameson never made it to the real battlefield.' She gave me a little time. 'What terribly bad luck for him.'

'And Jameson now, Mrs Underhill? Mrs Hudson seems fond of him.' The deep eyes turned to me.

'He has a good friend in Mrs Hudson. And she, I believe, in him.'

We sat on, looking towards the river in the distance.

'Chetwynd and Weir won every year because they could afford to keep two old deaf horses just for the Race,' she said. Another minute passed. 'I've been calling you Jack since I met you. I really think you should long since have been addressing me as Sarah.'

CHAPTER SIX

IT WAS MARCH 15TH, LATE IN THE EVENING, when I saw Harry and Edward next. They opened the door, frozen and shattered, the wind howling in past them, and collapsed on the floor. Outside were their packs dark against the snow, and the rifle. I trailed all in. They had got nothing. They drank a little sugared tea, and fell onto their bunks, still wrapped in the blankets in which they had been walking. While they slept I opened the packs. There was the tent, and the remains of the hide mat which had once been used as the floor of the tent. There were knife marks where strips had been slashed off, and tooth marks along the edges. So much for the caribou. Even though I had told myself I expected nothing I had somehow also, a secret even from myself until this moment, retained some hope they would bring something back. Like my belief that spring would come to the North on May 15th. What a foolish state I had been brought to by weakness.

In the afternoon, while Harry slept on and on, Edward told me a little of their terrible walk.

'The only thing that made sense was a journey as far upriver as we could go.' I could see Harry mouthing the words to him. 'They were not here, so they must be there.' Oh, yes. They'll be there, for a certainty. 'And where the caribou would be there might be musk ox, the easiest shot of all to take. They just stand and face you, Harry says.' At that Edward looked towards the bunk where Harry slept, but there was no movement. 'We set off the next day after Harry got back with the extra ammunition.'

'When there was nothing to shoot...' I looked into his face, hoping to see sense in it. '... why did Harry come so far back for more ammunition?'

He looked down and I thought he wasn't going to go on. Then he said,

'Because there was going to be a great herd. Several great herds... Anyway...'

'And the snowshoes?'

His hand rose and fell, to shut me up. 'Snow was falling and visibility down to a few feet. In minutes I had no idea in what direction we were heading, but we kept going. We stopped in the afternoon and managed to light a fire and had tea and sugar. In a break in the snow Harry saw a raven. That meant there were caribou, and on the move.'

'It did, did it?'

'For a certainty, Harry said. We crossed a lake, for easier walking, and came back onto the river. The wind was unrelenting. Even on the lake it took us four hours to make a couple of miles. We saw no tracks. No signs of anything.'

Edward drank his tea for a little. This was the most talking any of us had done for a long time.

'We found a little clump of spruce. Even Harry hadn't known it was there. We ate some of the hide matting for the first time, but neither of us slept from the cold and from the need to keep the fire going. We knew we couldn't go on, even if we had seen caribou tracks. If we didn't turn back to the cabin right away we would never see it again.' What would Harry have talked of then? 'We took wood with us and took turns beating the trail, and made tea and ate sugar and chewed on strips of the matting. That night it was the same again. No sleep because of the cold and the need to keep the fire going.'

'Why didn't you take turns at the fire, while the other slept?'

'The next day,' he went on as if I hadn't spoken, 'a real hurricane of snow and wind blew up. We spent the whole day in the tent. Yesterday morning we set off knowing that if we didn't make it back here by nightfall we would die on the trail. Neither of us could last another night in the open.'

He stopped talking, looking into the stove.

'We have had such bad luck with this appalling weather.' I felt like laughing, for a half breath. 'It's the circumstances: the coincidence of the caribou changing their path and these storms.' He stopped again and seemed to think, but I knew better. 'Perhaps it's God's will, to teach us a lesson. Perhaps some day we will understand it. But we know it's nobody's fault.' Not the fault of Harry? Your superior officer, Edward, whose orders must not be questioned? Oh no. All I felt now was rage. 'We have to take these things philosophically.' It rose and rose in me, rage that he was the fool he was, much greater rage that Sarah preferred this fool to me. And then he mentioned her name. 'I worry about poor Sarah of course, coping again on her own…' Before I could make my response he went on. '…but it's Harry I'm most worried about. He insisted on carrying the heaviest pack. And he fell, not once but several times.' The words I had saved for so long were out of me before I had thought it through.

'Sarah and I were lovers, Edward. But she chose you.'

He turned away towards Harry. Maybe his head went down a little. 'Perhaps he opened an old wound.'

'She chose you, you clown. If she was still mine I wouldn't have left her to come to this shit hole.'

'I have recovered.' I could hear him breathing steadily, heavily. 'But poor Harry seems still out of it.' I don't know what reaction I expected, but it wasn't this.

'I'm an adulterer. You don't want to hear that, do you? It's not done, is it? It's not gentlemanly. I'm a liar too, but not about this. I'm a thief as well. I stole your wife for a start. I doubt if I was her first lover, and I don't believe for a minute I'll be her last. Some one of your heroic friends in Footner, not fool enough to follow that clown up here, is likely enjoying her at this minute.'

There was a silence. Then, still turned away: 'Jack... we are all at the end of our tether.'

'Were you a coward in the War? Is that why you're here? If you were I forgive you. For you are only a poor human stick like the rest of us. But then, are you human, Edward? Or are you a bloody saint?'

'I am still sorry you came on this expedition, and didn't take my advice.' He sounded so sincere, and untouched by me. 'You could have avoided this suffering.'

Suddenly, again, I wanted to laugh out loud, but again I didn't. I had no idea if he understood me. Maybe I had waited too long, maybe the anguish of what lay ahead had driven away any pain a past betrayal might hold.

I left him there, keeping the fire going, keeping an eye on his cousin, and I went out and by some freak, for as usual I could hardly stand and my hands were shaking with cold and weakness, I shot a ptarmigan that was pecking near where we had searched in the dump. I took it back and we cooked and ate it right away, crunching up the bones and all parts of it, Harry eating in the mess of his bunk, and lying down again to sleep right after. None of us had anything we wanted to say now.

TUESDAY 3RD SEPTEMBER 1918

'Charles Dunae and his wife are not coming back.' I held in my hand the telegram Jameson had brought me an hour before, as if I'd have to confirm what I was saying. The telegram that told us nothing we did not know already. We stood looking down over Sarah's orchards, waiting, her taking a breath, holding it. Everywhere around us the land was a fading dull brown beneath the hard blue of the midday sky, everywhere except her acres. Here were the dappled green and red of the apple trees, brought to ripeness and colour by endless labour and endless sun. 'Somebody will come and collect their property.' I felt I should say encouraging things. 'Then the Company will appoint another manager. He'll free up money for roads, for piping, for ditches. For what's needed here.'

She leant a little towards me, in a way that reminded me of her friend Susan leaning towards her on Victoria Day, and saying softly, 'I'm not sure I ever did.' Her lips close to me, she said, 'Do you think, Jack, there is any money left to free up?'

She was waiting. I shook my head.

'And you know what's needed here as well as I do. It's not just more roads and piping and ditches. It's more rain. It's less sun. It's less howling, freezing winters. You haven't seen our winters.'

'I can guess,' I said. I hadn't heard her talk like this before.

'The wind comes all the way from the Barrens.' Her hand rose to point. 'Tearing down the Fraser Valley and along the Thompson. It gives frozen hell to everything.' She swung around. 'You would know it by looking at the trees. Everybody's trees.' A long breath escaped her. 'How was it in the Okanagan?'

I wanted to walk away, but I had to say something.

'It was less. Less drought. Less harsh winters. A little less.'

'And the soil?' she said. 'Better soil?'

'I wouldn't say that. In places, maybe.' What little I had said was true. 'These irrigation ditches will work. The flume will hold together. The worst won't happen. You won't have to give the place up.'

She didn't reply. I could feel her breath, her presence. Then, 'Is that the worst?' She took a step away, then another. 'How we planned what to do with the rest of our lives, once, Edward and I, in Wheathampstead, reading brochures from the Colonies.' There was a little breeze, barely cooling, rippling the leaves around the apples, rippling shade over the ground beneath. 'Brochures full of promising photographs. We liked the BCHEC's pictures of this little Eden in the wilderness. We both did.' We stood on, looking at the leaves ripple, shudder, the apples nod. This same sun and same breeze that was already drying out the moisture from the fruit. The apples were as ripe as they would ever be, and would not grow larger or with more flavour, would not become more worthwhile, but only begin to fall and spoil. 'When we got here these trees were shorter than I am. The BCHEC had used photographs of the Okanagan.'

She fingered a leaf on the tree nearest to her. 'Being superior hasn't worked out for us, has it?' The leaf had a shrivelled edge. 'Do you think your horticultural oil spray has worked out?' She toyed with the leaf again, let it go, ran her hand over more leaves with brown edges. I reached up and took an apple and twisted and it came off easily in my hand.She was watching me. 'You are right. The sooner we get pulling under way the better. The Chinese boys are still on BCHEC wages. They can pull. Pullers from Ashcroft or Savona might be got in, for those who can afford them. But it all costs. I shan't have any help. Except you.'

'Maybe you should spend the money.'

'Don't you know yet? I don't have money.' Into my head came those large houses in Wheathampstead, of the hunters, of the governess. I must have smiled or something, for she said, 'It's primogeniture, Jack. The law. Edward is the fourth son of a foolish father. And my father was a vicar. There is no family money, no remittance, for us.' Her head rose to indicate the land around us. 'Our money is all here. You appoint the Chinese boys where you see fit. I, Mrs Hudson, some others maybe, will pull for each other in turn.'

We walked away, on that early afternoon, down in the direction of the house, and the winding Thompson, walking through those fragile rippling acres of colour that she and her husband had put up over the pale brown earth.

'And let's look on the bright side,' she said. 'Charlie Dunae's left the Gray-Dort behind. I'm taking it. All I need is gasoline. Maybe he left some of that as well. Now: let's get on with it.'

MONDAY, 9TH SEPTEMBER 1918

A democrat, the seats taken out, and partly filled with Jonathon apples, stood by the orchard gate, the shafts propped on a water butt. She stood on one of the short stepladders, tipping in more apples from a wicker basket.

'There: done.' She threw her arms out and up in the air. 'For now.'

She stood, shoulders raised, the basket dangling over the wagon. The smell of the apples, ripe, rich, a few crushed, filled the evening air. She was smiling, flushed from work.

'You seem happy. And tired.'

I was tired myself. I'd put up a prop on the flume, and come back here and worked for two more evening hours pulling at first with Simon and Mrs Hudson, and then alone with Sarah. On the ladder above me, the hem of her dusty work dress, the dirty scratched boots with their fine stitching beneath the dirt, were close to me.

She nodded. 'Yes. I am happy.'

'So you should be. It's a good crop.' For the circumstances, for the age of the trees, it was a good crop. I nodded at the wagon and the apples, as if really thinking of them.

'It won't be long before we begin to sort and pack,' she said. 'And label and sell. And so it goes.' The wicker basket dropped from her hand and fell amongst the apples.

'And for you a rest. But I'll be at the flume and ditches till the end of time. Or the end of the War. Whichever comes first.' But I was smiling too.

'You will never get out of here,' she said. She laughed, still watching me from the top of the steps, and at that I knew my smile broadened. How long had it been since I had even thought of getting out of here? Suddenly I realized I had been thinking for months now that a place I worked in, none of it my own, was my home. I felt my face redden with embarrassment. I could suddenly see my naivety. I didn't want her to see it too, and I turned away. I put a hand over into the apples, and picked up one, and felt it, round and red and firm. I brushed my thumb across it, seeing the surface shine even more, a deeper red beneath where my thumb had passed. Then I said at least part of what was in my heart:

'I don't want out of here.'

When I looked up she was looking down into the apples on the wagon and not at me at all. Maybe she had not even heard me, and that was fine with me.

'There's some damages,' she said. 'I'll save them for the horses.'

She leant out over the wagon, then lower, stretching out, kneeling with one knee on the side board. She went further, then her hand supporting her among the apples slipped and she fell forward.

There was a peal of laughter.

'I'll damage the apples,' she called, but the laughter went on. 'I'll damage the apples.' And she rolled over on her back, her boots in the air, and made no effort to get up. She held up a hand. 'Help me,' she said. 'My good man: help the lady up.' I stepped onto the ladder, and knelt on the edge of the wagon, the board hard and sharp on my knees. I reached out. I was not close enough.

'Come here.' But she only waved a hand at me, fingers open, still out of my reach. Then she stretched out and caught my fingertips. She pulled, and I toppled forward and was in the apples, beside her, almost on top of her.

'You'll destroy the apples,' she said. Still she laughed. 'The apples.' She was looking up into my face. I was inches from her. There was the tan of her skin, the fine lines from working in the sun, the warm scent of her, the white teeth, her lips. I ached to kiss her. She stopped laughing, looking back into my eyes, quiet and serious. I moved closer, slowly, a fraction from kissing her. Then: what if I did, and what if I had miss-read this... what if it wasn't the contrived situation I thought it was... and she sent me away? I rolled over and sat up. Even as I did so I felt an ache in me. What a fool I was.

'We have to watch the apples.' Beside me she was sitting up too. I rolled over to the side of the wagon and got out onto the ladder. When I looked around she had already jumped down from the other side and was out of sight. When she came around the end of the democrat a moment later she was composed. Her hand was on the back of her hair, replacing a hairpin.

'How silly of us,' she said, cheerily, as if nothing really had happened. 'We were like big children. However. Enough. I'm off to warm up something for supper.' And with that, still fiddling with her hair and the long pins, she set off in the direction of the house. I stood there and watched her go, thinking I was a fool to believe she might have wanted me to kiss her, that I was a fool not to have kissed her anyway.

THURSDAY, 12TH SEPTEMBER 1918

The day we became lovers, but I was foolish and in that state already. In the short early autumn evening we were walking on the benches above the Thompson, Hector running beside us.

'I so wanted to get away from the apple pulling,' she said. 'I wanted to get out of Mrs Morrison's orchard and run home. I suppose that was terrible of me.'

'You could tell them you weren't well. They wouldn't know any better.' She turned to me quickly. I guessed I had spoken too easily of lying. She turned away again, and held up both hands, looking at the palms. They were clean hands, not especially darkened by the sun, but there was rough skin and blisters from raking and digging and pulling. 'The devil and idle hands,' I said. I held out a hand, dark and stained and rough, beside hers. 'We are angels.'

She dropped the blistered hands and turned to me. 'I wanted to come home and take a bath and sit on the porch and think.' We walked on over the short sage. There was a stillness and silence all around us, the sky full of those slowly drifting high clouds that would not break until far away. In this clear air darkness would soon come. 'Once I had enough time to myself to think. Now... except this afternoon maybe... I don't want leisure to think.'

She was smiling but it was a sad and tired smile. 'I wanted to neglect my duty,' she said. 'We go on wrestling to get water to the orchards, struggling to pull and pack the apples, fighting to get by here while our husbands and fathers and sons fight and die for something else, somewhere else.'

I walked on with her as so often, not knowing what to say and saying nothing.

'Of course I miss Susan Fellowes,' she said after a while. 'I could be less reverential about the mores of Footner with her than with anyone. Maybe because she didn't come to Footner with the intention of staying. She came on a visit, and ended up married to her brother-in-law's best friend.' She fell quiet after that, and we walked on. 'No. It was the kind of person Susan was that made her my friend. That and my need for a friend.' When she said nothing more I looked away, and up towards the far and dark hills, and that strong blue sky. We were walking slowly west, upriver, and the town lay around the bend. I had been at ease, but not any more, for she was not.

'I last had a letter from Edward three months ago when he was on a short leave in England. He told me about his visit to Westminster Abbey. There was an Active Service Postcard a fortnight ago: I am quite well. I have received you letter dated... Letter follows at first opportunity.' We took another dozen steps. 'I haven't been able to talk of him either. The wives of Footner don't talk much about their men, except of course about honouring them. No one talks much at the apple pulling anyway. Perhaps because there are other men there.' I heard her sigh. 'Even if some of them speak Mandarin, and the rest are deaf or nearly so.'

She stopped, and we stood looking down into the dark valley of the Thompson. The tips of two or three pines on the long narrow island far below were glowing golden in the low evening light, very still and quiet-looking, everything around them lost in deep shadow.

'I've known the people of Footner since the spring of 1914. I've known them with disasters and triumphs, with floods, drought, sunshine, crops, horses. With cricket and football and rugby and golf and running races and leapfrog and hockey and the hundred other sports we had before the War.'

We stood for a moment more, and then we moved on again. Her upper body was moving towards me and away, rhythmically, as we walked, and then she stepped closer and linked her arm on mine.

'No. I have known them all my life,' she said after a dozen steps. We kept going, over the rough bench land, and all the time all I could think of was the closeness of her, and of her arm in the sleeve of her Donegal tweed jacket pressing against me. I could almost taste her, her breath, her presence, and it came to me how all that physical longing had been there at our meeting on the riverbank in Kamloops, sitting beside her in the Gray-Dort, waking the first morning in the bunk-house. I ached for, longed for, wanted her, then and for every minute since. And what was she feeling, now, at this moment, at this touch of our arms? I wanted her to be as much in desire, in love, as I was. Because if she wasn't then it would not be love.

We wound around that long bend, and there before us, in the last of the light, were the first of the houses of Footner. There we stopped, still linked, and stood looking towards the pointed roofs of those surprisingly small houses, their wraparound porches, their fenced gardens with their starved roses, their short, empty streets lost in darkness. Lights were on at the Hotel. Lamps were lit in some of the houses. Not many.

She called to Hector. He came and sat at her feet. She took her arm from mine and bent and ran her hand over the dog's head.

'It's been a long day, Hector,' she said. 'I need to go to bed.' She straightened. 'I need to go back,' she said. Yet she stood where she was as if thinking. Then she linked her arm into mine again and leaning against me, in the near darkness, we walked away from Footner and towards her house. Our house, I thought, as we kept walking. It feels like our house. Neither of us said anything more all the way back. To our house, somewhere there ahead, beneath where the stars hung.

And maybe she had some such thought too, for as we came into the yard the grip of her arm linked on mine tightened. She stepped up onto the porch and opened the door and stepped inside, taking me with her. There she let go of me, and turned and closed the door behind us, shutting the dog out.

I could barely see her in the darkness of the hall, only the paleness of her face turned towards me, the white collar of her blouse beneath the tweed jacket. The paleness of her hands moved, more of the white blouse became visible. Then she stepped forward and put her arms around my neck and pulled me to her and clasped me tightly and kissed me.

And it was wonderful and astonishing and yet I had known all along that she would do this. I had known it on the riverbank in Kamloops, in the Gray-Dort, in the bunkhouse. On the banks of the Thompson tonight. I had been right about us, right after all. I had been right to stay.

I kissed her, my hands inside her open tweed jacket, feeling the roundness and firmness of her body, pulling her to me, smelling her hair, the warm scents of her, the feel of her cool cheek against mine.

'Christ... Christ...' she said.

I could feel her trembling, trembling close to me.

'Sarah. Sarah. Sarah.'

Then her tongue was in my mouth, and we were kissing and kissing, and then she stepped away from me, and I could make out her hands in the darkness pulling off the tweed jacket. I took off my jacket, Edward's borrowed jacket, and threw it on the floor. I saw her hands against the whiteness of the blouse as she pulled and pulled on the buttons until it tore open, and then she stepped closer once more and pressed herself tight against me.

FRIDAY, 13TH SEPTEMBER, 1918

The morning. The first next morning. I was on my back, my eyes closed. I could feel her warmth against me, her body against my left side, before I even knew I was awake. There was silence in the room, and then as I awoke further I was aware of the soft sound of her breathing. I opened my eyes. She was in my arms, turned towards me, her head on my shoulder.

With my right hand I moved a strand of hair away from her face, the better to see her. 'Sarah.' It had happened, this wonderful, changing, thing. It could not be undone.

My shoulder and arm were numb, but I would not move them.

Then I woke up suddenly, aware I had been dozing again.

She was standing by the bed in the morning light, naked, her back to me, one hand raised to the curtain at the side of the window, looking out at the brown hills. I could not take my eyes from her. I moved slightly and the bed creaked.

'You will be late for work,' she said. 'You have the Billinghurst's ditches to open.' She didn't turn. Her hand came down from the curtain and to the dressing gown on the chair beside her. She picked it up and, still looking away from me, put it on. I felt a chill at that moment. She tightened the belt, and turned back. 'You will be late,' she said again.

'I don't care.'

Then she leant forward and kissed my forehead. There was something sweet and lovely about it.

'You've never been late. You mustn't be late now. Up.' And she tugged at the sheets, tossing them away from me. 'Nor I for the pulling of Mrs Morrison's apples.'

'All right.' But I lay there, naked, still watching her.

CHAPTER SEVEN

THREE OR FOUR DAYS PASSED. At first I waited for his reaction to what I had said: readying myself for an outburst of violence, long bitter words, for something. When I looked in his notebook he had written only of the temperatures and the failed hunt. All seemed as before, except I had fired my little weapon of bitterness and hatred, and acquired no relief in return.

'Why did you leave her?' I asked him. We were sprawled in the snow and taking turns to chop in the frozen earth with a small hand axe. 'Leaving a woman like that alone for so long.' Goading him. It was his fault. He had the axe in his hand at that moment, but I had no fear of him. 'When she wanted you. You fool.' When I thought he wasn't going to answer he said,

'I was one of the last to enlist. It meant the end of everything, and I knew it.'

'Why, then? Why enlist at all?' As if I was the one to ask that.

He made several tired chops at the ground with the axe, stopped again.

'Some men said they enlisted while drunk. Or to kill Germans. But those weren't the reasons. They went because of pride, for love of their country. Because their pals went. Or those are the reasons I went.' He raised the axe, let it fall again. 'I went most of all because it was easier to enlist than stay and face the things that were said about those who didn't.' He rested. 'What alternative was there? To run away?' He raised the axe again. 'And you, Jack? What about you?'

I took the axe out of his hand. I chopped at the ground and said nothing.

Later, as darkness fell the wailing of the wind began to grow in volume and pitch. It would rise into a shriek, then slump suddenly into silence, then rise and scream over the cabin again, a bombardment of wind. But could anyone, even in Flanders, be as certain of death as we were now? Too weak to cross the room, the skull showing beneath the skin in all our faces?

Edward and I sat across the table from each other, leaning on our hands, slumped.

'Edward. You know we are going to die?' There was no sense of torturing or provoking him; but I had a craving, before it was too late, to have truth in this terrible place. 'Edward, I'm scared out of my mind at the thought of what awaits all three of us.' He sat up, leant closer. He was looking at me directly, as he seldom did. His hand closed on my arm, squeezed. There came the sound of Harry moving under the blankets, and Edward took his hand away again. Harry pulled down the blankets, abruptly, surprisingly, and sat up, looking around the cabin, his head swivelling, fingers opening and closing.

'Tea, Harry?' said Edward.

The terrible pallor on the scabbed gaunt face, the filth of him, the beard wild, the eyes wilder. There was a great explosion as the wind changed direction and struck the door. His head jerked to the side.

'It's all right, Harry,' said Edward. 'It's all right.'

'I've been in worse spots than this. In Old Fort Reliance I was down to my last cup of flour...' There was the throb and grind of the wind over the end of the tin chimney. 'And I pulled through that...'

'And you will again, and all of us.' Edward reached out and took Harry's filthy hand and squeezed it. 'So let us stiffen our sinews. Let us.'

In the midst of this world of make-believe there was a lull between the howls of the wind. With an enemy to provoke, more at ease now, I said quietly into that lull,

'It was the Indians who saved your life, Harry. They returned and fed you.' I leant towards him. 'That was what brought you back from the edge of death in Old Fort Reliance.' My voice began to rise. 'I was told that in Edmonton. There are no Indians here, Harry. There is nobody here to come and save us.'

'Look... we all feel rotten,' said Edward. Conciliatory Edward.

'We don't feel rotten... we are dying...' I yelled it at them both with what energy I had. Then I left it there, for already I did not want to say anything more about our position. It wasn't Harry or Edward whom I didn't want to hear it. It was I at that moment who could take no more truth. I nodded, as if someone had said something wise and real.

'There's a man,' said Edward. 'Pluck, if we have enough of it, will see us through.' I couldn't bear to look at him.

SATURDAY, 28TH SEPTEMBER 1918

No one came to collect the Dunae things. No one at all had come from the BCHEC. The crate Charles Dunae and I had carried in so long ago still sat in the Dunae barn, one side open, a water pump visible. The Gray-Dort stood beside it, Sarah having driven it twice, taking the Major to and from Dr Reynolds in Ashcroft.

My images. That's all they are. Flick, flick, flick.

We had loaded the Fellowes' democrat at the rail station with fence pots and wire ordered from Kamloops to save money, and were about to drive off when Mrs Bennie and Isa turned the corner towards us.

'The Bennies,' said Sarah, watching them. 'She'll be wondering why we didn't buy this from her cousin's store. Because it costs more, and he just orders it from Kamloops anyway.'

'Mrs Underhill. Mr Butler. What a fine Saturday morning. You're keeping Mr Butler busy, I see.'

'Mrs Bennie. Isa,' said Sarah. I nodded at them.

'I see from the *Sentinel* that wonderful things have been happening on the Hindenburg Line,' said Mrs Bennie. 'The Third Army is advancing.' There was a silence.

'That's lovely, Mrs Bennie,' I said. 'Had you heard that, Mrs Underhill?'

'No, Mrs Bennie.' She was watching Isa fingering one of the fence posts in the back of the wagon. 'I have been remiss, I think, in my recent following of the War.'

'There has been a breaching of the Wotan Position. So Miss Weir tells me. I hadn't heard of the Wotan Position. Eleanor's always very up-to-date with news.'

'I'm sure she is,' said Sarah. 'I'm sure she is.'

'We've been missing you at our afternoon teas, Mrs Underhill. We haven't had your company for, what... well, some time now.'

'Yes, Mrs Bennie. I shall join you again soon. I promise.'

'Those teas are such a link with our old lives.' Mrs Bennie turned to her daughter and they smiled at each other. 'We so look forward to the return of the life of the pre-War years.' It had the air of a remark that was frequently made between them.

'We should get home now, Mrs Bennie. Perhaps you could drive off, Jack?' said Sarah. I went to hand her up into the seat but she was already climbing there. I followed her and gathered up the lines. 'Good day,' she called.

'Good day,' I called.

We turned onto Centre Road and were leaving town.

'The War could go on for as long again,' I said. I wanted it to. Maybe I was the only one in Footner who did. 'With places like this keeping old Britain going.' She was looking steadily ahead. 'Like all the Colonies. Steel from Canada. Wheat, beef from Canada. Timber. Shells for the guns from Canada.'

When I thought she wasn't going to speak she did.

'And men from Canada,' she said. 'But even more important than our men, our apples.' There was something harsh in her voice. 'The War effort is being kept going with our Footner apples.' She turned to me, and said more softly, 'But all will never go back to how it was before the War. Nothing will ever be the same, ever again.'

Which pleased me. Of course it did, but there was nothing I could say, and she was silent too, all the rest of the way home.

SATURDAY, 5TH OCTOBER 1918

Evening, our lamps as yet unlit. I stood by the parlour window, looking out towards the darkening talus slopes, thinking of what I had here in this little town, in this house, with this woman, while I waited for her to finish bathing. She came up behind me and put her arms around me and pressed her naked and scented body to me. Wheathampstead, I thought. Some English village in some English county, far from here. Where Edward is welcome to return, welcomed by his family. Welcome to stay. While I have his wife. While I take his wife to bed. I tried to imagine that young man in the photograph thinking like this, doing these things, that slightly squinting, smiling face saying those words. He never would. All the more fool he, then, for only someone who thought like this, was like this, could make a woman like Sarah happy. Someone like myself. That was why she was with me. That was what I thought, then.

Or the next morning, as we lay late in bed, wrapped around each other, and I told her, and meant every word of it:

'No painting, no tree, no sunset, no piece of music, no writing was every more wonderful, more beautiful than this: your wonderful, beautiful naked body. What clowns artists are, musicians, writers, anybody who praises rainbows and flowers and storms and oceans instead of this. Or fool priests and ministers with their ideas of the miraculous... have they never...' and my arms tightened around her and almost shook her, '...have these people never held a naked woman in their arms?'

It was a joke, and yes, I meant all of it.

Or later that same day, sitting at the table having tea after a walk on the benches overlooking the river, her hand coming across the table and covering mine. In kindness, in affection. Maybe even, for all I knew, in love.

'That first evening, over tea and cake, when you produced your bedraggled loaf...'

I shook my head, as if embarrassed. 'No.'

'And the next morning...' Her fingers tightened and squeezed. 'I lay on in bed that morning, knowing you were at the door, looking in. I had heard Hector bark. If you had stepped into the room then, come to my bed... I don't know what would have happened. Yes I do: I would have taken you in. I wanted that. What you would have thought of me, what the consequences would have been... I would have dealt with that later.' How lovely she was, her head tilted, thoughtful.

'So I lay there awake that morning and my hand over my face to conceal it, waiting... waiting for you to cross the bedroom floor, and put you hand on my shoulder.' Why hadn't I? 'And I listened to you searching my house, knowing you were about to leave, going into the recreation room, where I'd hardly been myself since Edward left... I came to see you there, but the moment had passed.'

'I didn't leave.'

But I didn't say: 'I will never leave you. Wherever you go, I will never leave you.' I didn't say 'You are my everything.' I didn't say 'I love you'. How could I, when I was waiting for her to say those things first?

'No.' Her fingers squeezed again. 'No.' Her hand went away, back to her tea cup.

THURSDAY, 31ST OCTOBER 1918

Yet afterwards I could still wonder how we could have between us wasted all those months of summer. This wonderful thing we had, instead of being over almost as it began, would have been had for longer, and built on, maybe to last all our lives.

Yet what I learned on that last day of October 1918 seemed to change so little. It was momentous in the instant, yes, but even she seemed to forget about it quickly. Or maybe it was only I who forgot about it quickly. 'Our lives', as I thought of them when I could have meant only 'my life', went on, thousands of miles from Europe, on the bench lands of the Thompson.

I unsaddled Sam in the little corral behind the bunkhouse, gave him hay and water and a handful of damaged apples. I was stiff and sore from hauling and lifting timbers and from riding. I took off the worst of the dust in the bucket of water by the corral. I stood there feeling the coolness of the water on my skin, the dust in my mouth, in the air around me. I tasted it with my tongue on my teeth and lips. I turned towards the house.

By the time I had taken a dozen steps I'd forgotten about the dryness and grit, for over the sweetness of the bruised apples there was the smell of food coming out to me on the still air. I was suddenly, overwhelmingly, hungry.

Yet it surprised me. When I left in the morning Sarah had been going to work all day sorting and packing and labelling apples in the Hotel ballroom. We would have eaten some cold meat and bread in the evening and it would have been fine. But clearly she had come home early, and cooked food. There would be conversation while we ate, then her washing the dishes, I chopping wood for the range, filling the water tank from the Jimmie. I would tell her my news: Wang Chi and his crew were leaving in a week, now the apple pulling was over. And then we would sit together in the parlour. And then we would climb into that heavy mahogany bed and she would wrap her body around me.

These were the ordinary and wonderful things I was thinking as I flung open the door and called, 'Sarah.' There was no reply. I took off my dirty boots and walked on in and up the hall and there she was, at the range, Hector at her feet. The pans were on the range, the plates and knives and forks on the table. 'That's good.' I could feel the saliva form in my mouth. 'It smells really good.' She didn't turn. 'It's been a long time since breakfast.' She put boiled potatoes into a serving dish. She covered it with a lid. I didn't know what was wrong.

'It's ready,' she said over her shoulder. But there was something wrong.

'Riding that pony takes more out of me than the work.' I watched her, in the steam, her sleeves rolled up. She turned in my direction but didn't look at me. She put the covered serving dish and then another on the table. 'You came home early from the apple packing?'

'Sit,' she said. 'Please.' She took off her apron and rolled down her sleeves. She sat across the table from me, and uncovered the other dish and put a chop on a plate and passed it to me. 'And vegetables.'

I spooned potatoes and carrots out onto my plate.

'And for you?' I held out the dish.

She shook her head. I ate, and after a while she took a potato and carrots and put them on her plate and began to cut at them. It was clear that she was not eating but only moving pieces of food around. I put down my knife and fork. If this had been me I would have wanted nothing asked, so I asked nothing. After a few moments she stopped the cutting and pushing and put down her knife and fork. She clasped her fingers together. A moment passed and then her head rose.

'Edward's been wounded,' she said. I looked back at her, trying to read her expression. Him.

'Badly?' The empty cypher, as I moved about his house, ate at his table, slept with his wife.

'I'm not sure.' She shook her head. She sat on, the hands clasped. 'Jameson came this morning with the telegram. And of course, the minute I saw him coming onto the porch I thought: it's Edward. Something has happened to Edward.' Her head tilted to the side. Had she wondered was he dead? Had she hoped… what? 'I went to the packing anyway, because what's to be done? But I had to come away.'

'He'll be in a hospital well behind the lines.' All I was really thinking was how this might affect us.

'Edward's in England.'

'Yes?'

'Yes.'

'Will he… get leave and come home?'

'Nobody comes home to Canada from the War. You know that. He'll either die and be buried in England or he'll mend and be sent back to France.' We sat on in silence. I was thinking of the one-armed Midge Andrews. And Fiske, with his crutch and his empty trouser leg. And all the other half-men I had seen across Canada. They had come home. 'It just said his wound's in his upper body.' Her hands opened. 'That could be anything.'

The empty cypher was in the room, and she was upset about his suffering. Her husband's suffering. That surprised me, foolishly.

'He'll be safe then, for a while. For months maybe.' Or he might die. She was looking back at me now, her lips tightly closed.

'Yes,' she said. Her head shook. 'No.' Then, 'There is a bread and butter pudding on the range.'

Her head went down again. As she sat on I could see tears move slowly on her cheeks and fall to the table, and yet she sat there. 'I'm sorry, Sarah. It might well be a light injury.' And then he would be back at the Front. And all would be as it had been. But he might also be dead even as we sat here.

Then her right hand came across the tablecloth towards me. I reached out and put my hand over hers. The touch of her skin under mine excited me, and my fingers began to close, my thumb to stroke the skin on the back of her hand. Then her hand turned over, and we were palm to palm. Our fingers closed, and became interlocked. Her fingers were tightening. Then her fingers loosened and her hand withdrew. I tried to read her expression, but her head was still down. She rose to her feet, her hand to her mouth.

'Excuse me,' she said, and walked quickly away. I heard the sound of her bedroom door open and close. After a minute I rose also and walked quietly in my stockinged feet to her bedroom door. Hector was there before me, his head to the side, listening. I put my ear to the boards. There was what I expected: the sound of sobbing.

I went back to the kitchen and cleared the things away. Darkness had already fallen. I would not look around and see what jobs were to be done tonight. I filled a bowl with some of the still-warm bread and butter pudding. I went out to the porch, Hector following me. There I sat in the darkness, my head full of what had happened. I didn't eat all of the bread and butter pudding, and put the bowl down for the dog to finish.

After a while I rose, and Hector following, walked around the house to where I could see the bedroom window. A light shone from it. I stood for a moment, uncertain. Should I go to her? Or leave her alone? What would she want? I went back to the porch and sat there in the darkness for another while, sometimes patting the dog's head, all the time looking up at the night sky and thinking about her, and what might happen.

I rose once more and went around the side of the house. The bedroom window was in darkness, the light gone. I went inside at last, and undressed, and slid into the big bed beside her. Then she turned to me and we made love and all was as it had been. How ridiculous I was.

FRIDAY, 8TH NOVEMBER 1918

The sun still with some warmth, the morning air so fresh… this was a good day. Another good day, beginning. I would go in soon and kiss Sarah one more time and eat breakfast and ride off to work. And some day soon, on a good day like this, I would tell her that we had to plan a future, to make this last forever.

I picked up a stick from the dirt and held it above Hector's head and he leapt for it and I turned and turned and he followed and followed. I kept turning, on and on, the dog following, jumping, the stick always just ahead of him, and I felt the air pass cool on my bare forearms, and cool on my shaven face. And I kept turning and the dog jumping, until I was dizzy and toppling to the side.

Hector leapt and got the stick in his mouth and tugged it out of my hand and made off with it towards the house. The hills were swimming past me, the dotted pines a blur, the house, the hills, the house, and then it all started to slow and I could focus again.

I stood there looking at what I had not seen the day before. Along the crest of the furthest hills lay a thin line of white. In the night snow had fallen there, or had been there yesterday and I had not noticed it. This was early snow, and would go away, but more would come, and that would not go away, but creep down those hillsides, and on to our hills nearby. Then to the ground beneath our feet.

Yes, each day had been so long and slow and full, and yet the winter had come so quickly.

MONDAY, 11TH NOVEMBER 1918

When I saw Mrs Morrison riding out that Monday evening, coming out of the darkness and calling for Sarah as she dismounted, I kept on walking from the corral to the wood pile. Then I stopped. Edward. He had died of his wounds. Or he was on his way home, too ill to be nursed and sent up again to the Front. But wouldn't Sarah know of that first, by Jameson, with a telegram? And Mrs Morrison's expression… it was open-eyed, and bright. There was joy in it. What it really was never entered my head.

Sarah came out onto the porch, the lamplight behind her, drying her hands on a tea cloth. Mrs Morrison stepped up and took her arm, and they went inside. I stood there in the darkness, leaving them to it. I was still there when Mrs Morrison came out, walking slowly, looking behind her. She got back on her horse and rode away. I took a step towards the house, my arms full of logs, and Sarah came out, one step, and then another into the bright cold winter night. At the sight of that shocked face, her pale cheeks, I stopped. It had been about Edward. He was dead. It would be all right. She came on again, gazing at me, until she was eight or ten feet away.

'The War is over,' she said. Just like that. Standing so still, open-eyed, open-mouthed.

'What?' But I knew what it was. For every other man, woman and child in Footner it was wonderful. And for her? For me?

'The War is over,' she said again.

'That will be good, then.'

'Yes. Yes.' So quietly. 'Of course it's good.'

She wasn't looking at me any more, but past me into the darkness. I thought she was going to say no more about it.

'Edward will be home.' I would say it if she wouldn't. 'He'll be coming home.' She kept looking past me. Some of the logs fell out of my arms.

'Yes.' She looked so calm, or immobile, anyway. I saw her take a deep breath. 'I'm glad it's over. I'm glad he's safe.'

Why didn't she say: never leave me? Why didn't she say: I will leave this farm. I will leave before Edward gets here. We will go west. Start again, on some quiet place on the Island, with milk cows and a goat, with chickens, with two fruit trees for ourselves, with a little boat for fishing. We will start again.

I stood there as if she might say something like that, but she said nothing more, and I walked on, and dropped the rest of the logs somewhere at the side of the house. I heard a couple of shots, then a half dozen more from the direction of town. Then a rocket rose from that same direction, and another and another. Far-off cascades of silver and golden stars fell to earth, and faint crackles and bangs just after came on the still air. Then more.

The bunting from Victoria Day went up across Centre Road for a while, the Union Flag flew from the Hotel, but little changed. No soldiers came home. The soldiers of Footner were almost all officers, and were doing important things in Europe. No one seemed to know what it was they were doing in Europe. They would not be home until February, some said, and others June or July. If Sarah knew anything different she did not say it to me, and we went on as before. To me it was as before.

Then a gale from the north blew down part of the bunting and it wasn't put up again. On Christmas Eve a party was held in the Hotel. Some residents had left for the holiday. One or two visitors had come, but Susan Fellowes wasn't among them. I went to that Christmas Eve party, because Sarah had asked me to, because her friend wouldn't be there. Maybe I went because I was insecure and jealous. I arrived ten minutes after her, in that practised way we had now.

She was standing near the door of the dining room, talking to one of the visitors, a florid man in his mid forties. Beyond her other women sat in small groups around tables. Elderly men talked and smoked, and three or four boys and girls stood silently. At the far end of the room Major Sidgwick sat with his little coterie of listeners. The piano, violin and clarinet played Good King Wenceslas.

I came closer to Sarah, eavesdropping, so I suppose I was insecure and jealous. 'I'm not married myself, Mrs Underhill,' the florid man was telling her. He leant closer, his eyes fixed on her. She was nodding.

'Yes?'

'Yes, indeed. And both my parents are dead.' People passed us, chatting, chatting. 'Alas, yes,' the florid man said. 'Both of them. First my father. His heart, you know. Barely a year later my mother went.' His tongue came to his lips and wet them. 'A woman's ailment.' His oiled hair had been grown long at one side and combed over the bald crown.

'I am sorry,' said Sarah.

'One doesn't like to talk of these things, but then, you... well...' I came a step closer again. You are wasting your time, I thought. Sarah is taken. She is taken by me. She was looking back into his eyes. 'With a woman...' he was saying. 'With a woman a man can talk about these things.'

'Yes,' she said. 'Tell me more about your parents.'

But he needed no encouragement.

'My father was always so active too. Played cricket as well as tons of golf. Skated when in season...'

A child of forty. I moved on into the room.

Miss Weir was waiting for me, ornate black armband still in place, smiling that tight smile. The life-sized portrait of Gordon with the black crepe ribbon still on the wall behind her. The framed map of western Europe gone. Her concession to the armistice, to victory? 'A drink, Mr Butler? A beer, surely?'

I shook my head. 'I'm not much of a drinker, Miss Weir.'

'No? Then… tea?' She half turned, a hand out, towards a table where plates of small sandwiches, slices of Christmas cake, mince pies, waited on plates. Ladies of Footner sat near that table. Behind it stood a Chinese waiter. A stranger. 'Many of the ladies are taking tea.'

Suddenly I wanted tea. I wanted tea and sandwiches and cake, and peace and quiet and calm regular things, and no thoughts of the endless flume and the desert and the isolation and the aftermath of war. I nodded, and followed her. Miss Weir poured tea, offered plates. I took a salmon sandwich. 'You are a big working man, Mr Butler. More than one surely?' How solicitous she was. I took another. She offered slices of Christmas cake. I took one, and a mince pie. 'My, you are hungry, Mr Butler.' It was pleasant. I was out of my depth, but it was pleasant.

'Thank you, Miss Weir. Thank you. This is most pleasant.'

'Ninety cents, Mr Butler.'

'Of course, Miss Weir. Of course.' I paid her. The waiter put out more small sandwiches and more Christmas cake. Behind me I heard the florid man. 'Sparky,' he was saying. 'Sparky…'

I took my cup and saucer and plate to a chair to one side. The piano, violin and clarinet played O Come All Ye Faithful.

'I've always so enjoyed our little evening soirées,' Mrs Bennie was saying. 'We have to keep them up. One thing I have regretted has been the absence of young friends for my Isa.'

'Young people will return, Mrs Bennie,' said Miss Weir. 'From now on we can certainly return to life as before.' Beside Mrs Bennie, Mrs Hudson sat quietly over her tea and mince pie. Without her black armband. 'Or it may well be better,' Miss Weir went on. 'I've heard that a lot of great friendships have been established over there, with the men bonding together. I wouldn't be surprised if some of the chaps brought their new pals back here with them, and we have even more of a wonderful little town than before.' How much of this did Miss Weir believe?

'I agree.' Mrs Bennie.

'We have honoured our heroes by continuing the endeavours they began,' said Miss Weir. 'We cannot have done anything better for them.'

Others nodded approval. Mrs Hudson sat quietly, looking into her teacup.

'And your husband, Mrs Bennie?' Heads turned in my direction. 'Any word of his return?'

'Thank you, Mr Butler, but no. No recent news of Lieutenant Bennie. Not that I expect any.'

'And Captain Trip, Mrs Trip?'

'Soon, Mr Butler. Soon is what he writes me.'

'They will all be home in due time.' Miss Weir. 'Do you remember how we used to send parcels of warm socks and gloves off to the Front? All those things that took so long to reach them? And how we sent out crates of apples? I used to hear all the time how Footner apples were so well received.'

What did any of them really think? I finished my little sandwich and the Christmas cake, and started on the mince pie. The piano, violin and clarinet broke for tea.

'And we sent over books,' said Mrs Morrison.

'How we ransacked our shelves and hunted out the type of things we knew men liked to read, and sent off bundles for when they were relaxing.' Mrs Trip.

'Jerome K Jerome?' I offered. 'And Conan Doyle, and *Diary of a Nobody* and *Vice Versa*? And Wisden?'

'Why, yes, Mr Butler,' said Miss Weir. 'My own suggestion.' I was getting the smile now too. 'Wisden.'

I brushed off the crumbs and rose, and walked away to the other end of the room, where a young Engelmann spruce had been put up as a Christmas tree. Major Sidgwick sat close by, red-faced, talking with vitality to the three or four women around him. Near the door Sarah still listened to the florid man. After a while I saw her reach out and touch his arm. She led him across the room to where the piano, violin and clarinet players sat over tea cups. Sarah bent, spoke to Miss Ricketts, then the florid man, and left them together. Miss Ricketts in her plain navy dress and her light brown and greying hair in a bun. Sarah made her way to the bar, and picked up some short drink in a tall glass, spoke to Mr Fellowes—asking him about Susan?—and moved to a window, and stood there, looking out into the night. I came up behind her.

'You got rid of him then?' She sipped her drink. 'I wasn't introduced.' As if every word, gesture, emotion of Sarah's should be mine.

'No.' She didn't offer any more, nor turn around. Had she found something attractive in him, something I couldn't see? Was she wishing I wasn't here?

'Ah, Mrs Underhill… I'm not married myself.' She turned towards me, straight-faced, holding up her glass but not drinking. 'Call me Sparky. Everybody does.' I could see her lips tremble. 'Sparky. If you ever come to Ontario just ask for Sparky. They all know me.' She was biting her bottom lip. I waited for her to laugh. 'It's holding it back that makes it worse.' As soon as I said that I knew I had made a mistake.

'I'm not about to laugh,' she said abruptly. 'Jack, he's lonely and has no idea, and never will have, how to do something about it. Mrs Cook is his only relative. Who travels to here from Ontario to spend Christmas with a cousin they have met just once before?' Her voice fell. 'He will end as he is now, having sat out his life in frustration.'

'Well…'

'His last good years gone.' She took a breath, and spoke more softly still. 'He hasn't even been to war and experienced the comradeship that Edward writes me, in the midst of all its evils, he found there. '

The cypher had come into the room. I looked away. At Major Sidgwick, with his little coterie of listeners. At the women in small groups around tables. At the elderly men in their groups and the three or four boys and girls in theirs. I looked at the florid man leaning forward, talking animatedly to the silent Miss Ricketts, clarinet and violin leaning back, keeping out of it. Telling her no doubt of his dead parents, of his forty-year-old orphan state, of his desperate loneliness. I was looking at them but I was thinking of Sarah, by which of course, I realized later, I meant myself.

I have chosen to remember that time as seldom thinking of Edward, but of course it was not so. A prevarication.

I would be in her bed and she in my arms, and I might think suddenly... if that bedroom door opened now and Edward walked in and saw us and gasped I could only welcome it. For then it would all come to a head, a decision would have to be made... how could he still want her after that? How, after that, could she choose to be with him and not with me?

But he didn't walk in, and he never found us like that.

He found out in other, maybe no more subtle, no less cruel, ways.

Weeks went by, then a month. There was still little rain, and what there was fell as snow or sleet, for the temperatures dropped further. I found jobs in the Dunae yard, for there was no one to tell me not to, or I'd ride along the flume, hands inside the pockets of the same heavy Harris tweed coat of Edward's that Sarah had worn driving from Kamloops to Footner, stopping off to do only the most necessary repairs. The thermometer at the Hotel porch, glanced at as I came home at the end of the day, would read 30° F, or 26° F, or at its lowest, 20° F.

It was only when the wind changed from the south-west to come howling down the Fraser Valley from the north, making the temperatures drop another ten or twenty degrees, bending and loosening the weakly rooted fruit trees, making the pipe over the Thompson swing wildly, making the water surge in the flume, sweeping the supports out from under it, that I saw the real destruction of the winters here. How terrible it seemed after the long long summer. Mostly I spent little time dwelling on the past, and less again on considering what might be to come. I knew what I had now, and that was enough.

On my weekends in February I pruned Sarah's trees for suckers, downward-growing branches, competing leaders. Like everything else I knew about apple trees I had learned this in the Okanagan. The other orchards would have to go another year without pruning.

In late March I moved into a room in Mrs Hudson's house. This was Sarah's suggestion. Edward might arrive back any day, any night, maybe with little warning. It wouldn't look good if I exited an hour before he arrived. Tucking my shirt-tail in, she said, and we laughed. I minded, but it was for the best. Of course it was. Neither of us seemed to think it a good idea that I move back to the bunkhouse. Most evenings I'd tell Mrs Hudson I was going up to play cribbage or some other card game with my former landlady, to whom I still owed hours of labour anyway. It suited us both. In the mornings Mrs Hudson and I would pass toast and tea over breakfast and say nothing at all to each other of ourselves.

So there were less nights in Sarah's bed, but there were still nights. I was letting myself believe that this was how it would be from now on. Even after Edward came back this was how it would be, somehow. I believed that because to face the truth was more than I wanted to bear. I was in my fool's paradise, and happier there.

CHAPTER EIGHT

THAT NIGHT HARRY SLEPT QUIETLY. The next morning he began to talk of going out to where we had slaughtered the caribou at the end of February. All that day he talked about it, and on the next, April 2nd, he said he felt he had rested and was well enough. He staggered off, despite Edward trying to stop him and offering to go himself, and came back hours later with a block of frozen snow and blood in his hands.

'I found this,' he said. 'This will make an excellent snack.' He put the red and white lump of snow on the table, and took out his old bone-handled knife. I put in my mouth what he handed me, until the snow melted and I could taste the blood. All the next day he rested, and on April 4th he said he was going out again. He could hardly stand upright.

'It's madness, Harry,' said Edward.

'When I come back I'll be crocked,' said Harry. 'Whatever happens. I'll be all in. You have to carry on.'

'Rest more, and I'll go out instead, Harry,' said Edward. 'And Jack would too, I'm certain, if not for his foot.'

By midday Harry was leaving, muffled up in blankets, taking tottering steps, falling over, righting himself, going on. He didn't even have the rifle with him, being too weak to carry it. I despised the man, but I had not his will and his domination over his body, and nor had Edward. That afternoon Edward and I fried up bits of fish bone and gut, and waited, while the poor fool tottered and crept and crawled his way across the snow, seeking bones gnawed by wolves long ago.

'How can he cross the drifts?' said Edward. He was sitting with a fish spine in his hand. 'How can he bear the wind? He will be on his hands and knees all the way.' He put the fish spine in his mouth and crunched it. There was no hurry to speak. 'Harry is not a man, but something more.' Then, and when I expected, 'Mustn't lose pluck, old boy,' or some other of his banalities, he threw me again, and said, 'I've known Sarah all my life, Jack. I expect she's told you that.' He crunched and crunched and swallowed. 'We were childhood friends. Then later I had to prop her up over various boyfriends. She'd get her heart broken so easily.' He stopped, looking down at the mess of bones. 'Poor Sarah. And then there was this Irish chap.' Was this going to be some reference to myself, in Edward's oblique way of talking about what mattered? 'He came to the house as a manager to the estate, even though he was so young. Had a good farming background, but he never looked strong. Not robust, you know. And she just fell for him. They used to sing together. I'd hear them, off in the woods. Never could sing a note myself. Couldn't join them there. Irish songs sometimes. I'm sure Sarah has told you all this.'

Of course I knew nothing of her Irish lover.

'He died. Tuberculosis. I think we all knew it was on the cards from the beginning. What must it be like to be in love with someone and know it will never come to anything? That you will never have a future with them?'

What answer could either of us make to that? He turned towards me, and looked into my eyes.

'That's when I knew I had fallen in love with her. Strange isn't it? All those years as children, but it was when I saw how she loved and mourned poor Michael, saw her tear herself apart over him, that I knew how I really felt for the first time about her. That I loved her.'

And I, with my petty little physical idea of knowing her.

121

'She quoted Byron to me… I suppose she's done that with you as well? Something about a woman's love being her whole existence, but a man's love for a woman is a thing apart?' I said nothing. 'But she was wrong.' He coughed a little and drew a deeper breath. 'She is my whole existence. That's the way round it is, you see.' I found myself nodding. I understood. 'But I know how it is with her. I know how she loves me.' How he watched me. 'She loves me like a big brother.'

I believed him. I wanted to.

'Edward.' I don't know why I said what I started to say next. 'What I told you before…' I was going to tell him I was lying, that I had been jealous of his marriage, of his farm, of anything. I didn't care. There was enough pain in this place already. Then I knew he wouldn't believe me if I told him it was a lie. He was just a poor in-love broken thing, another loser, like myself, and deserved better. Or maybe I just saw him as not a threat any more.

'A dear big brother,' he said. He rose and began to scrape together the fish bones.

Later Harry was back, hobbling up to the door, falling inside. He lay there until Edward made his own slow way to him. He tried to help him rise, but in all his thick clothing Harry was too heavy for that. After a while he got to his knees himself. His forehead was still touching the earth floor. 'There. I crept around in circles, around…' He stopped. Time passed. 'Wolves must have got it.' With that he got to his feet.

'There will be a break in the weather soon,' said Edward. 'There must be. You have done all you can, Harry. You couldn't do more.'

'All my emotions seem played out in me,' said Harry. 'All of them.'

MONDAY, 31ST MARCH 1919

We stood, my Sarah and I, at the edge of the bench lands, looking down into the shadowy Thompson. A mildness in the air that spring evening, a relief after the cold that had been on the land since autumn.

'Remember us at Twin Lakes last year?' Her short tweed jacket, a toque hat, a little dust on the boots' toes beneath the long straight skirt. Her closeness to me. 'How warm it was. What a happy summer day.' I nodded. 'When Susan was here.'

'A happy day.' It seemed so far away. Everything before we were lovers seemed far away then. But I had only known it was happy as I sat beneath the flag pole with Hector and watched her and Susan Fellowes and listened to them talk, and the bats had come out, and the day was already over.

'For you too, Jack?' I nodded, anyway. 'I'm glad. Because I loved it. Except at the very end.' I waited. As I waited I did a boyish thing: I had a stone in my hand and I tossed it out over the river and saw it arc up into the evening light, begin to fall, and then vanish as if some other hand had snatched it away. 'Because then I lied to Susan.'

'Yes?' She could still surprise me.

'Yes, Jack.'

I waited.

'I told her the thing to do was to stay on here. Because it was our duty.' She looked up, across the Thompson, to the north shore, to the road, to the flume, all invisible there. 'Let's go to the house. Get indoors. Before you go back to Mrs Hudson's.'

I expected her to take my arm, but of course she didn't. Someone might have been riding in the last of the light in the hills behind. Some CPR man walking the line. Someone high across the Thompson in the darkness on the road from Kamloops to Ashcroft, an impossible distance away. Yet she had taken my arm and we had walked here, linked, once upon a time.

THURSDAY, 24TH APRIL 1919

And those last weeks went on, and we kept meeting, different to how it had been of course, but in its own pattern now. And then, on the day a year since I had met her, one of those meetings, different again.

I stood alone on the north shore of the Thompson, at this rare reachable beach where we had picnicked and paddled and lain back in the sage and juniper, Sarah and I, in a summer so already long gone. A little evening breeze from the west, warm and good. I turned my face up into the breeze. The sun like honey, she had said then. 'I can feel the weight of it. The weight of the sun.' How the sparkle of the water had hurt the eyes. And Hector in the water, and her wading in to save him. Would always, she said. Her little bare pale feet. These stones in front of me had known her feet. The burning sun, the smell of the sage and juniper, the wet hem of her dress, her bare feet on the stones, her fear of the Thompson. Flies dancing like motes.

The shadows were long from the benches opposite, just reaching this small stony place. The sun had come back strong already, and would come hotter again to here. We would sit again, if not here then somewhere else, her and her dog and I, and talk and eat and be, unstated, in love.

Then I heard the sound of a horse behind me, and without turning I knew it was her. Yet I didn't look, in case I was wrong. But a moment passed, and the horse stirred, and the rider did not speak, and so I was more sure again it was her. Watching me, watching the river, silent and breathing and close.

'On the snag,' she said. Still I didn't turn. It was what it had always been, the two of us talking about some aspect of the apple trees, of the weather, of the river, of ourselves. 'See? On the snag,' she said again. 'The poor beast.' I turned.

In her tweed jacket buttoned up. Her husband's cap. Her pale horse. I turned back, and there it was. A snag in the river, a fallen pine caught in the shallows further down. The dark carcase of a cow, low in the water, jammed against the snag, only the fat swollen belly and raised legs to be seen. I stood and looked. The cold and heat took and coyotes and cougars took. The land took and if not that then the river took. It just seemed wrong to leave it there. 'We could put a rope on it.'

She shook her head. 'It's not coming out of the Thompson until what's left of it's in the Strait of Georgia in a month's time, smashed through Hell's Gate, gnawed at by god knows what on the way.' I turned towards her again. She was looking not at the snag and the dead animal at all but over her shoulder, to where the night was already on the hills and where the clouds were darker and more coming quickly. 'Let's ride up,' she said.

I followed her from the little beach. 'Do you know what today is?'

'The cinch is loose,' she said. She pulled Cap to a halt and dismounted and put her hands to the big strap. I dismounted as well and let the lines fall and stood behind her.

The wind was rising, raising the dust of the dry coffee earth around our ankles, this warm wind from the west. There she was, the scent of her, the scents of her body from the ride, from the dry gusty evening. There were the scents of horseflesh, of the leather from the harness, blowing past, and gone. There was the whip of her hair, loose in places, lashing, falling.

I was closer to her without knowing I had moved closer. Her tweed jacket, that jacket she had once stripped off and flung on the hall floor, was inches, an inch, from me again. Then my hand was on her back and she was turning and her arms were around me, and the horses and the cinch and the wind were forgotten, and she kissed me.

She took her lips from mine. 'I know what today is,' she said, and kissed me again. I threw down my coat and we lay on it. This frantic, hurried thing. All wonderful, all beautiful whether frantic or slow, all bringing to me what only love-making with her ever did. 'Quickly,' she said. 'Quickly.' Then it was over, this hurried, hungry thing. I stood up, and pulled my clothes around me. She lay where she was, arranging her petticoat and skirt. The rough ground, the stones, sharp tough low shrubs, had torn at my hands, must have hurt her too, and the wind of the evening was on my naked skin and on hers, but I was smiling. I stood there, tightening my belt, grinning. Then seeing her face, I looked away and around as if for the horses. But I knew where they were, grazing ten or twelve yards away, lines trailing.

She was on her feet, picking up the tweed jacket, when I saw them, out of the side of my eye. The young Collingwood boy and the Durant girl, on ponies just beyond Cap and Sam, stopped, looking straight at us. What was in their eyes? Puzzlement, I think.

'Good god.' The terror in her voice. How open-eyed, how shocked. Then, 'Andrew and Jacqueline!' she called, in a cheery assured way. 'How good to see you here. But away out here? You must be going to the little beach by the river. But it is getting late.' She was walking towards them, putting on the tweed jacket as she went. 'You will be careful down there?'

She stood with them, talking quietly now, her hand on the lines of the Collingwood boy's pony, pointing back once, not to me but to the ground nearby. Then she held up a hand, and turned and started towards me again. Then she turned to the children and called: 'That little beach has no name. Juniper… would that do? Juniper Beach?' and came on again to me. Together we watched them. But they turned their ponies and walked them off in the direction of the Savona Road. They were well away before either of us said anything.

'What did you tell them?'

Her hand went to her hair, pushing it back from her forehead. Now the children were gone she was a lot less assured.

'That we were looking for a ring I had dropped.' She swallowed.

'And they… said what?'

'They nodded. They agreed.' She turned to me and watched my face. 'I think it will be all right.'

I watched the children ride on home, to tea, to mothers and grandparents and friends. And what would they say to mothers and grandparents and friends?

'Did they ask if we had found it?' She said nothing. 'The ring?'

'I don't think they'll tell anyone. They believed me.'

I took a breath. I didn't care. I couldn't make myself care, right now.

'I'm sure that's right.' I was smiling again. 'Two children… what would they understand? And so what would they say?' I took her arm, and we moved towards the horses. She was walking quickly, pulling ahead of me, and like that, her getting further and further ahead, we rode back towards town.

Then just before we were to part, she pulled Cap to a halt.

'Of course they will tell,' she said. 'Because there are two of them, and they will talk it over until they came to some sort of understanding, and then, because there are two of them, they will race each other to be the first to tell it.'

She waited for me to say something, but I had nothing to say, and she turned Cap and rode on home.

THURSDAY, 1ST MAY 1919

Men had come back, men to whom I nodded and had nothing to say, who had no experiences I wanted to hear about. Welcome home parties were held in the Hotel, which neither I nor Sarah attended. Some came with damaged bodies. Some, wounded and unwounded, left soon after, taking wives and children or sisters or aged parents with them. Reggie Fellowes was one of these. But Edward had not come back.

I was walking in Mrs Cook's small orchard in the late morning, a notebook and pencil in hand, marking up what irrigation ditches needed to be re-dug for the summer already on us. It was as if I had no intention of doing anything else, that the bright and hot and dry days would continue and I would be part of them. I put down the notebook and pencil and set to pushing a collapsed fence post upright. Deer had trampled down the wire and come through looking for fodder among the trees. They would eat the young shoots as they came on the branches. I was busy keeping dying Footner alive.

There was no call from her, just the sound of hooves on the hard road, but I looked up and there she was coming towards me. Sitting so straight, gloved hands on the lines, the Donegal tweed jacket and cap, dark hair tied back. There was a whinny, and the horse stopped.

'Sarah.' I called it louder. 'Sarah.' I dropped the fence post and took quick steps over the dusty earth towards her. 'You found me.'

I could see her head moving in little nods. It looked as if she was trembling, but Cap was pawing the road, and that could have been the movement of the horse.

'Perhaps later you would come up and take a look at some things for me?' She wasn't smiling. It hurt. She was taking so much for granted. 'When you have finished your day's work.' I stopped walking towards her. We were a half mile from the nearest house, a dip in the land hiding us.

'Why don't you get off Cap?' She could come to me. She could let me kiss her. Yet she sat there, high above on the horse, and her trembling, saying these things about work. 'Is there an orchardist hiding around here somewhere?' I looked around, held my open hands out. She didn't smile or laugh back or make any movement. '"Come up and take a look at some things for me"?'

I could see her lips move, but I could hear nothing. They moved again. 'Come and see me,' she was saying.

'I'll be tired tonight.' I wanted her to bother, to show she wanted me. 'I might not come.' But I was also thinking about the smooth skin on the inside of her thighs and the curve of her lower back and the feel of her hands on me.

Her head fell. Then she looked up again. She put the side of her hand to her eyes and took it away again.

'Jack. Come tonight.' It was loud and unsure at the same time. 'Just come.'

'Of course I will. About seven? About seven?' I said it louder, as if she might not have heard me.

'Later,' she said. 'Eight thirty.'

I nodded once. She sat there looking back at me. I could have taken those other few steps. I could have reached up and pulled her off Cap and held her in my arms and said, 'What's the matter? What's happened?' It wouldn't have changed anything. There was nothing that would have changed anything. Then she stopped looking at me and leant forward and shook the lines and clicked her tongue and moved away. I watched her go, along to the fork that would take her back home or the road into town. She took the road into town and out of sight.

What would she be doing in town? Maybe picking up something at the station: a parcel of books, mail, some clothing from England. Visiting the shops. But the general store, the haberdashery, the butcher's, would be closed by now. Then to talk with Mrs and Miss Bennie, with Mrs Scott, with Mrs Trip and Mrs Collingwood, with the other ladies of Footner, over tea at the Hotel with Miss Weir. I had never known her do that. And what would she talk about with them? I only knew what she talked about with me.

After a while I walked back and picked up the notebook and pencil. I did not see her go home again.

About seven o'clock I poured warm water into a basin in my room at Mrs Hudson's place. I washed slowly, thinking of Sarah. Soon I would hold her in my arms and look into her eyes. Already, just thinking of that, I felt my whole body open out to her. I would kiss her and kiss her. I thought of what she might be doing at this moment. Also washing, probably, at the washstand in the small bathroom. I thought of that, picturing her splashing water in the heavy basin, a trickle flowing between her breasts. She would part her legs to wash there, looking at herself naked in the oval mirror. I shaved, knowing that soon I would be putting this smooth face between her breasts and between her legs. I would spend the night with her, warm and content, in her soft feather bed, and we would make love again before I slipped away at first light.

At about eight o'clock I stepped out of Mrs Hudson's house onto the silent dark street. I passed Charles Dunae's deserted property, and walked quietly and quickly on. I could smell the shaving soap from my skin in the still cool air, my face tingling as I came over the crest of the hill and past the last of the houses near town. To the east all was already dark, but towards the Coast Mountains the sky still had a trace of orange and red across a hard metallic blue. A single star hung there. On far peaks beneath that star lay terrible cold and deep snow, on many all through the summer. But here, in the dip in the land that sheltered all but the pointed roof of her house from the sight of the town, sheltered it too from the worst hard winds of winter, lay only warmth and softness and pleasure.

There was one light visible, shining behind the blind of the parlour window. I walked up to the back door as always, and in the shelter of the porch turned the door handle and stepped inside. She was sitting in the leather chair as I expected, under the light of the tall brass lamp on the desk. She didn't look up. She had a book open on her lap, and continued to read, as if eager to finish the page. Then she closed the book and raised her head. She reached out a hand and I came forward quickly, and bent and put a hand behind her head and kissed her. For that second there was no response, even as my lips were on hers, and then she kissed me back, as always.

'Shall we go to bed?' I said softly into her ear. She shook her head. Then she put her cheek beside mine as if to kiss me again, but didn't. I never thought her more beautiful than when her face was close to mine and her breath in my mouth. She pressed her cheek to me, and I felt her swallow. I was impatient. 'Why not?'

'Why not,' she said, and kissed me after all, and we went to her bedroom. She was undressing quickly, and then stopped. She raised one hand to the open curtain, and I thought she was going to pull it closed, but she instead stood in the starlight looking out. I couldn't wait. I stepped up behind her and took her in my arms, and pulled her towards me, my hands over her breasts. She half turned. Then instead of kissing or speaking her eyes fell, and she stepped away from me and continued to undress quickly and turned down the covers and got into the old-fashioned bed almost as if she were cold.

When I got in we lay side by side and held each other, and I looked down along her naked body so close to mine. I knew this was, as it always was, a truly happy moment: the anticipation of making love, with so much beauty still ahead. The anticipation too of that oblivion, that exclusion of all else, like a great deep unconsciousness, that nothing but making love with her had ever brought me.

And we made love, and maybe I was blind and dumb and only a man, but I knew nothing then or could think of nothing later that was different, except maybe she was more quiet and intense than usual, those same quiet and intense ways that along with her beauty had made me first feel I loved her.

I wish...but then to wish to have understood more would be to wish myself somebody else.

Afterwards we lay back, her in my arms, her head on my shoulder, and I was tired and happy. Like in the first days, when I could hardly believe she was with me, I didn't want to sleep this night but to lie awake and be aware of the wonder of it all. She seemed to fall asleep quickly and deeply. Then I awoke suddenly, and knew I had been asleep after all, and looked at her, turned half towards me, a hand near her head, hair spread across the pillow. I lay there looking at her, but sometime after that I must have slept again, for when I woke next the half moon had come around enough to be seen through the window, and Sarah was lying face down, her head turned away from me towards that window, her body clear of the sheets. There was a sheen from the moonlight on her naked back, and the curve down to her buttocks, and then the darker shadows and hollows of her body. In this light from another world I was struck suddenly with what a precious and precarious thing this beauty was.

'I had a letter from Edward today,' she said, without moving. I flinched back from her before I thought. 'He is in Montreal. Or was when he posted the letter.'

I had to clear my throat before I could say anything.

'What does that mean? He's coming home?'

'He's coming home.' There was a trembling in my chest. 'You knew he would be coming home.'

Into the silence I said eventually, stupidly, 'Then how will we meet?'

'We won't, Jack.' She turned over at last, and lay on her back. From habit and desire I put a hand on one of the breasts, silver in the moonlight, my thumb from habit and desire stroking the dark nipple. She put her hand on top of mine and moved it down to her stomach.

'How will we meet, Sarah?' I sat up, propped on an elbow to look down on her. Her eyes were open, but she was looking away from me and towards the window and at the half moon hanging low over the bare hills. Even then I was taken aback by how she looked in that cold light, and I began to feel desire again. But I couldn't touch her like that now. 'All right. It can't be as it was but we can still meet.' I took a breath and held it, waiting to hear what she would say, wanting her to say, 'Yes. It will be difficult, but we can still meet. I was wrong. I judged it too harshly. We shall still meet.' She said nothing. The breath left me again.

She got out of bed slowly. She stood beside the bed and took the long cotton nightdress she wore when I wasn't with her from the back of the chair. She put it over her head and struggled with it, but the rest of her was naked, and she tugged again and the nightdress came down the rest of the way and the silver body in the moonlight disappeared from me. I was tired suddenly.

'I deserve better.' What if what she was saying was true? Or worse: if she wanted it to be true? 'I wouldn't treat you like this.' I remembered then standing in the orchard and saying that I might be tired this evening, that I might not come. What a fool. I could feel tears coming to me, and I didn't want them. I was still a fool, propped up in her bed, her and her husband's bed, sheets over my legs, while she stood next to me, looking out of the window at her struggling fruit farm and telling me it was over. 'But I'm not wanted now. Am I?'

I got out of bed on the other side and began to dress. Behind me I heard the mattress give as she sat down. I had my trousers and shirt on, and I turned round. Her head was down. I could hear her breathing, more heavily, haltingly.

'Is it my fault, then?' but I said it softly.

'It's only that Edward is coming back, and I can't see you again.' I could see her swallow after she spoke.

'There are other ways. Other places. In the Gray-Dort. Along the river bank…'

'No.'

'Among the trees…'

She turned and looked at me, the first time since she had fallen asleep with her head on my shoulder hours before. She hadn't been crying. She shook her head. If she had been crying then she would have looked weak, and maybe I would have bullied her and said angry words and slammed the door and called 'you bitch' at her and that would have made me happy, or at least at first happy. That was what I thought then. I got many things wrong then.

But she hadn't cried, and looked at me instead as if it just made sense, this imperative that what we had been these past months was over, and I would see the sense of it too, soon, or eventually.

I went around the bed and dropped to my knees beside her. I didn't care. I wanted her.

'Don't. For god's sake, Sarah. Don't make me leave you. I want to be with you, and not just in bed.' I didn't know if I believed what I was saying myself or not. 'There are other places we could go. There are other ways to live.'

She was turning away. I could feel my tears on my cheeks.

'This place, the whole town, has no future. A child could see that. You'll leave anyway. Leave with me.' I went to take her hands, but she kept them firmly on her lap. 'My doing these repair jobs... if there were a hundred labourers... it wouldn't make this work. We could go to Vancouver Island. There's farms and orchards there.' I would tell her anything, whatever it took. 'Workable, prosperous farms. I know people who have gone there. Or anywhere on the west coast.' I had lost her already. She said something, and I couldn't hear it. Whatever it was had to be better than no words, than this.

'What did you say?' I asked her. 'What did you say?'

'You haven't...' She fell silent. 'Why didn't you...' She stopped again. I had no idea what she was saying. I waited but there was nothing more.

There was the rustle of her nightdress, and then she sat up straighter, like how she rode Cap, like how she drove the Gray-Dort, and said,

'Jack, my husband is coming back. It has been good with you, but it has to end.' That clear voice, determined, with no weakness. I wanted to make a weakness. My bad angel wanted to find something I could yell at, a flaw to abuse her with.

'You must have known... how long?'

'This morning,' she said. 'Just this morning.' Her tongue came to her lips, as if they were dry. 'The last time he wrote he was still in hospital. He was to stay with his family...' She had known when she had spoken to me in Mrs Cook's orchard. She had known all day as I had worked, anticipating this night. While she had sat astride me, the base of her thumb in her mouth to stifle, unnecessarily, her little cries, she had known.

'And you couldn't tell me this morning?' My voice rose. 'Or during the day?' I had something I could blame her for, something I could yell at. As if that would make the loss of her easier. Yes. A fool. 'And we have this, and then... you tell me?'

'I called on you this morning so we could talk tonight.' How familiar that clear English voice was, speaking quietly. If there was a different tone to it from so many other days and nights I wasn't hearing it, but then I was a man, and Irish and dumb. I twisted the knife in myself, a little man. 'I couldn't tell you there, after all we have been to each other, at the edge of the road. Yet when you came into the house I didn't know how to tell you either.' After each sentence she paused, and there was coldness and terrible stillness in the room, and then she would speak again and coldness and stillness would go away. 'I kept looking at that stupid book of Edward's—a life of General Gordon, for god's sake...' She exclaimed at that, as if it was surprising or mattered. 'And I could think of nothing to say. And then you kissed me.'

'You had this with me tonight knowing it would be the last and you said nothing?'

'We can be friends...' Had she said that? Or had she said, firmly and steadily and coherently, 'I will be your friend. We will support each other'? But all I heard was the word 'friend'. All I was set on hearing.

'Friends? What makes you think we were friends?' I said it, hating what I was saying. 'I came here and fucked you when you wanted it, and you wanted it often.' As the words came out my voice rose, as if I wanted her sleeping neighbours, the other wives and widows and daughters and respectable ladies, old Willie the wagon driver, Major Sidgwick, all to hear it. I wanted her exposed, her secrets out, the word spreading to the Hotel and Miss Weir and beyond to England. The bitch Mrs Underhill has been having a lover in her husband's bed while her husband fought for his country. Then I would walk away and forget about her. The bitch. 'As I'm sure others fucked you before me and many will do after me. Your husband *Edward*—fuck you and your clown husband Edward. Whatever we were it was not friends.'

I finished dressing while she sat on the bed looking out into the moonlight, saying nothing. I pulled on my boots while still standing, not wanting to sit on the same bed as her, and went to the bedroom door and opened it, and stepped through, and paused before slamming it, hoping, wanting her to call, say something, anything. At any word, even the angriest word, I would turn back and, hurt and ugly and foul-mouthed as I was, take her in my arms again. There was only silence following me. I pushed the door half-heartedly.

There on the small table in the hallway lay the big gloves she had been wearing all that time ago on the drive from Kamloops to Footner. They were Edward's. And what she had been wearing today, riding Edward's horse: the tweed cap, the Donegal tweed jacket. Also Edward's.

'Jack,' I heard her call from the bedroom. She had said something. I stood there. Now she had called I knew there was nothing but a weary ache in my heart, made worse, not less, by the sound of her voice. I opened the door and went out and closed the door behind me. I had never had her. Everything was Edward's.

Somewhere far off to my right the new day was beginning. I had ditches to dig, dead wood to saw, weed clearing to do. The interminable flume to repair. I walked back down the road I had walked up as a blind fool hours before. I went in through the side door to my room in Mrs Hudson's house and, a couple of hours later, when Mrs Hudson, realizing I wasn't coming to breakfast, knocked on my door I called out that I was ill, and wanted to be left alone.

CHAPTER NINE

ON APRIL 7TH THE WIND DIED, although the cold was still terrible, and I went out to look at the trapline while Edward and Harry stayed indoors. When I left, Harry was talking again of going out and looking for the caribou bones. When I came back, not with any food but with a fallen branch I had trailed after me, Harry was still in bed, and asleep once more. He and Edward had eaten pounded bone, there being no other animal food.

On the morning of April 8th Harry ate some more of the pounded bone, but did not rise from his bunk.

'We have to find firewood,' said Edward. 'Sometime today.' He looked at the empty stove for a while. 'It's all gone,' he said.

'Soon. I'll go soon.' I lay on but couldn't get warm, and about an hour later rose and went outside without speaking to anyone. I was looking around at what was left of the black spruce when Edward came out and stood beside me. I could see the marks on several of the trees where he had attempted to fell them, and given up after a couple of strokes. I was supporting my weight on the axe handle. I couldn't fell them either.

'The cache,' he said. 'The furs don't need it.' He paused and breathed deeply for a while. 'We can build it again when we are well.' The pause and the deep breathing came again. 'When spring comes.' We took wood out of one of the side walls. The poles were thick and would last a while in the stove. 'We could take one more pole,' said Edward. But we just sat on in the snow and looked at the wall, for we had no more strength left. 'What we must never burn is the canoe.'

It took an hour or more for us to get the poles round and into the cabin. They were in a heap near the stove, and we were collapsed on our bunks

'We won't light the stove yet,' said Edward. The rasp of his breath went on. 'We will wait till Harry gets up.' I waited. 'Then we can boil up bones.' There were more rasps. 'Are you all right?' he said. 'Your breathing… like you are laughing…?'

'I'm all right. All right.' I began to drift in and out of sleep.

Harry did not rise again. All that night Edward attended to him. He lit the fire and made tea, and tried to get him to drink it. I would doze and wake up and he would be rubbing Harry's leg, or an arm, trying to massage blood back into it. There would be more tea made. Then, 'I shouldn't have come back, Jack.' I kept my eyes shut, but Edward's voice was quite firm and deliberate. 'It was a mistake. A mistake to be rectified.' I was thinking: if you hadn't come back I'd still have Sarah. Neither of us would be in this cabin. Then you left her anyway. 'There were all those good chaps I knew, Jack. So many. All good chaps.' And I realized it wasn't just coming back to Footner he meant. I opened my eyes. He was looking at me, knowing I hadn't been asleep, that I had been listening. 'They…'

Behind him Harry's hands clawed at the blankets.

'Too warm.' His voice was dry and rasping. 'Too hot.' Edward picked up a mug of tea but Harry did not take it. 'The sweat,' he said. He ran his finger around his bony neck. 'See the sweat…' The fire had died down, and the cabin was icy cold. Harry kept tossing about, with more energy than I had seen in him for days. 'Take off the blankets,' he said, his fingers trying to grip them.

An hour later he was asleep again, heavily covered in blankets, some of Edward's too I suspected, the capote spread over the top of them. His red-rimmed eyes were closed, his dark and withered lips clenched, his whole body shivering beneath his heap of clothes.

'I'm very worried about poor Harry,' said Edward. 'He was the fittest of us.' I felt, unexpectedly, the urge to laugh again. It was the other side of raging at Edward, that anger that was more and more pointless. After a while he said, still watching Harry, but speaking to me, 'What I was saying before, about the War: you come back, and you don't want to tell anyone, your wife even, perhaps your wife most of all, about anything over there. Yet when I told her nothing I felt I was lying… that I was saying there was nothing to tell. It would have been nice to move on, to just forget about it.' He stopped and sat for a while looking at Harry. 'But I can't forget about it. I wonder if you understand that?' I said nothing. 'Perhaps you do.' I had no intention of encouraging this idea. 'Could you imagine that? Lying to Sarah?'

But of course I understood.

The daylight was well advanced when I woke the next morning. When I opened my eyes Edward was at the table, writing laboriously in his notebook. I rose and lit the stove, and he cut strips off the caribou mat and put them on to boil. Everything we did took so long now. I was poking at a wolverine skull when I heard Harry's voice, quieter than usual.

'Death's like a fourth in this room. All I want to do is sleep. If I sleep now I'll not want to awaken. I have to write something.'

Edward tore a blank page out of his notebook and took it with the pencil to Harry's bunk. I pounded the skull between the stones, raising the stone and letting it fall, resting, breathing three or four times, raising the stone again, over and over. I was using Harry's tin trunk as a seat, and even through a blanket and my tweed trousers and woollen underwear it was hurting. As I rested I would look at Harry, held upright by Edward, the paper supported on the back of the notebook.

His hand seemed steady. He somehow managed to write a letter to Colonel Underhill. I read it shortly afterwards, when it had been left on the table and both of them were asleep:

Your son Edward is a perfect gem. I leave all my worldly goods to him, what I have now and anything I may come into. Our hardships have been terrible, and he has come through them bravely. You have every right to be proud of him. Had I lived I should have had a tale to tell of his hardihood, endurance and courage which would have stirred the heart of every Englishman.

Fool, fool, fool. After he had written this letter Harry rested for a while, and then,

'I have two more days,' he said. 'One, maybe.' How grey-skinned he was, the sores and scabs dried up, the bones of his face so visible. Even the dark beard seemed wirier and more brittle than before. 'You, Edward, are the best shot. There will be musk ox. There will be caribou. Soon. Birds will go over. Going north. Then you will know it is spring.' When Edward stepped back from him I wondered for one moment if he had died, but there was the rise and fall of his chest.

I was sitting on Mrs Hudson's porch, taking a long break, hating my jobs, hating everything, and not wanting to leave either. Or maybe, as Harry would say later, my emotions were all played out in me.

I watched Jameson getting off his bicycle and coming stomping onto the porch. He nodded, and left the *Inland Sentinel* on the chair beside me. Mrs Hudson, hearing the sound of his twisted foot on the boards, came out and picked up the paper. She passed it to me, while watching Jameson climb back on his bicycle and ride away. Every day Jameson left the *Inland Sentinel* on the chair, and every day Mrs Hudson came out to see him cycle away, and leave the paper unopened.

'Nothing, I expect, in there,' she said. I took the newspaper and waited until she walked away. Alone on the porch again I picked up the paper and thumbed through it as I would do had I been reading it. After a while I stopped pretending to myself and lowered the paper and looked down through the empty lots. A dog collapsed on its haunches in the middle of Centre Road scratched awhile and lay still, baking in the sun. Fiske, on his crutch, came from the direction of the old laundry and entered the Hotel. Beyond the dairy and livery stables two rail workers, Terry Sullivan and Albert most likely, lounged about in the shade on the CPR platform. The afternoon life of Footner. I watched it so I could be bitter and hate it.

Mrs Morrison left the dairy and walked towards the other stores on Centre Road. Last year she had stopped me in the street and talked of how long her husband had been gone. Three years. Three years without my husband, she had said. Now the husband was home, fingers missing, shrapnel in his back, but alive and seemingly hearty. There was her neighbour, Mrs Scott, coming out of the store. Twenty-three years old, younger than myself, coming up to me, back in the summer days, to talk among the trees. Her husband home too. There was somebody else with her, a younger again woman. Young lonely women. I had wanted only Sarah.

There was the sound of a motor car. I turned.

The Gray-Dort, Sarah at the wheel, coming into town on Centre Road. She wore the cream dress of Kamloops, the dress I had seen hanging in her wardrobe so often since, her hair under a large boater held on with a cream silk scarf, pale gloved hands on the wheel. She did not glance once towards the Hudson house. The bitch. I formed the words in my mind. The dog slept on, and Sarah steered the car around him. She turned sharp left before the drapery store and continued on towards the CPR station. I folded the *Inland Sentinel*, put it back on the chair and rose. I walked slowly to the Hotel. Major Sidgwick was on the porch in his cane chair.

'Good afternoon, Major Sidgwick.'

'Good afternoon, my young Irish friend,' said the Major. He turned his head in my direction. 'How are you today?'

'All serene, sir. All serene.'

'My son the Captain is coming home…'

'Yes, Major.'

I stopped by the doorway, standing back in the shadows of the porch. There was the Gray-Dort at the CPR station. The two fifteen Kamloops train, then. She was pacing up and down the platform, disappearing at times behind the cabin, appearing again. I would lean to the side, the sooner to see her, then there she would be once more, her cool pale iridescent figure. After a while she seemed to content herself, and sat quietly on the bench facing the line. I went into the darkness of the Hotel's empty bar. The brass foot rail was gleaming, the mirrors polished, the shelves and racks of bottles and glasses tidy. Only the unswept dust blown in at the doorway showed that some standard had slipped out of Miss Weir's control.

She came from the back herself to serve me.

'Yes?' she said, standing there, unsmiling, a pen in her hand, making a stranger of me.

'I would like a ginger beer, Miss Weir.' Her face kept the same expression. 'Please.'

'Ten cents.' I took out a dime. At a table in a corner Billy Fiske sat on his own with a glass of beer. She took a step forward, as if to get the bottle from under the counter. 'Twelve cents,' she said, straightening.

'Twelve cents?' I waited. She stood on also. Eventually I put my hand in my pocket and took out two cents more and put them on the counter. At that she came forward again, opened a bottle and put it and a tumbler on the bar. I picked up the bottle, and walked away up the broad stairs to the tables and chairs on the balcony along the front of the Hotel.

I sat there in my lonely splendour, rocking back in my chair, watching Sarah, unmoving, across the way, her back to me, in her pale straw boater, in the sunshine on the railway bench. What was she thinking? I looked at that pale hat, at its roundness, and thought of the dark hair underneath it. Of her underneath it. What pleasures was she looking forward to in the return of her husband? That he would leap from the train and into her arms? Back into her life. Back into her bed. I could feel anger rising in me. Was she worried about gossip getting back to him? But what did I care who knew? Maybe Miss Eleanor Weir knew. I hoped that many people knew. Maybe it had always been that way, my being proud that I, the blow-in from the Okanagan, from Ireland, had become her man. As proud as I was jealous of those I used to imagine had gone before me, those whose existence she denied but in whom I could never quite stop believing. The husbands and brothers who had gone to France with dear husband Edward. Served in battles with him. Captain Sidgwick, the Major's son? The dead hero Gordon Weir maybe? Bitch, I said softly. Bitch. If I said these things often enough I might believe them.

I wanted to hate her, for in hating her I would not want her any more. I would be free. But I did want her, right now, at this minute, even as the thoughts formed and trickled away and reformed in my head. I could hate her, but not hate her enough.

After five or ten minutes there was the hoot of the train far off, and a plume of dirty smoke. I watched the train and its two carriages and the line of freight cars come closer, and brakes and wheels grind and screech and the train stop. She got to her feet. One of the CPR men unloaded packages from the guard's van. No one got off. There was a burst of steam from among the engine wheels. Then at last a carriage door opened, and a slight man in a grey suit, a faint moustache, carrying a suitcase, stepped down. This the soldier, the Captain, the wounded hero, the husband?

I saw Sarah go towards the man. She stopped a yard in front of him. At this distance how frail and old he looked. He lowered the case to the ground. He and Sarah stood unmoving. Were they talking? It didn't look like it. Behind them the CPR train snorted and puffed. Then Sarah stepped forward, took the frail, old-looking man in her arms and hugged him. His arms did not rise to hold her. Fool. She would not have to wait for me to hold her. I kept watching, seeing his right hand rising to her shoulder. His head was beside hers, into the side of her neck. There was a humming in the warm air. I leant forward in the chair, as if away from the humming, as if to hear them. Was he telling her how he had missed her? How he loved her? Was he kissing her cheek?

They separated, and he picked up his case and followed her to the Gray-Dort. There was something about the way he moved, his left hand hanging by his side, that suggested it was of little use to him. I watched him put the small case on the back seat of the car. There was a stain on that seat, just about where you have put your case. A stain I made with your wife one night after we had taken the Major to Ashcroft and back, and on the way home parked above the Thompson under a nearly full moon, overcome with lust, warm beneath a thick red tartan blanket. What would you know of that, Mr Soldier, Captain, Sir? Have you ever, with her, with anyone? He bent and cranked the handle until the engine spluttered into life. When he straightened Sarah moved across to the passenger side. No, no, he gestured, pointing to the driver's seat. He climbed awkwardly, one-handedly, onto the passenger's seat. The motor car moved off along the road out of town and towards Sarah's place. Sarah and Captain Edward Underhill's place.

Had I been a drinking man I would have gone downstairs and into the bar and if Miss Weir had not sold me alcohol I would have climbed the bar and taken all I wanted. But I went slowly downstairs and out onto the main street, and back to Mrs Hudson's and to my room. I drew the curtain over the window, locked the door, and lay on my bed in the dull light for the rest of the day. I tried to sleep, but all that came to me was bitterness and hatred, and that left no room for sleep.

Eventually I realized from the fading light on the other side of the curtain that dusk was falling. Just four evenings ago I had been washing in this room, eager to walk the dusty road to Sarah's place. Now she was there with him. In my head he wasn't Edward but 'him'. Him, that man who had come to live with her. In those rooms, walking those floor boards, putting his bare feet on those rugs where I had been. Him, who would get into that big soft bed with her tonight, if they hadn't done so already, and every night.

I got up, left my room and walked towards the river. I stood there on a sandy ledge in the fading light, watching the water two hundred feet below, hearing it, catching a glint of the stars on it. There was an end to all pain, all anguish, all disappointment. An end to all hatred and to all love. One more struggle, and then no more. I stood on, thinking my sad and bitter thoughts. I became aware my limbs were stiff and I was shivering all over, with no idea how long I had been standing there. I was sadder than ever, but neither could I kill myself.

At that I set off along Centre Road and towards Sarah's house. The Underhill house. I hurried on, running at times, to bring warmth into my body, so I told myself, but it was a sudden hunger to see her again, with no idea what I would do if and when I did. Eventually I paused to catch my breath. Above, the stars were so startling bright, round and gleaming in the clear dry air. Jewels scattered on black velvet, I thought. What a love-struck fool. A jealous fool. I went on, making myself walk slowly.

I stopped only when the high roof of the house rose up in a black triangle against the stars. Another couple of steps and I could see the glow of several lights from beneath the porch roof. One was from the parlour window and one from the recreation room. Even from here I could hear the sound of a piano in the still cold air. It was some simple tune, and then became another simple tune, one I recognised as Für Elise. I came closer, and stepped up onto the porch opposite the recreation room windows.

The curtains were pulled closed and I could see nothing. I leant softly against the glass, but all I could hear was the sound of the piano played slowly, carefully. She was playing for him. She had never once played for me. I could see my breath on the cold air now. It would touch the glass, mist it over, clear immediately, then mist again. A late cold spell in Footner. Eventually the piano playing stopped. I heard a man's voice, but I could not make out the words. There were footsteps, and the light in the room began to fade. The lamp was being carried from the room. I moved along the porch towards the parlour and front door. As I passed the bathroom the glow of the lamp appeared there. I continued on. As I got to the parlour window the light faded from there also. It could have been no more than nine thirty, and they were preparing for bed. I went on around the porch, past the side door, pausing, listening, and to the window of the second, smaller, bedroom. It was in darkness. What had I expected? That Edward would sleep there? I went on, and looked in through the dining room window. The curtains were open but I could see no one, only the faint shimmering light of the lamp in the hallway beyond. I stepped off the wraparound porch, and hurried to the bedroom window. I had come right around the house, wilfully, foolishly, making myself believe all the way that perhaps this was not where Sarah and the husband she had not seen for almost four years were preparing for bed. The curtained window was already aglow when I got there. At this same window, four nights ago, Sarah had stood naked, looking out into the night, dropping the nightdress over her head, telling me this was the last time I would ever know her like this. I was glad the curtains were fully closed.

I listened, and could hear the low sound of voices, stopping, starting, as in a conversation. Then suddenly there was a laugh. Sarah's laugh. The man's voice fell silent. She had laughed at some joke he had made, and he was satisfied. In minutes they would be in bed, if not so already. Before they could turn out the lamp or pull back the curtains I made myself step back from the window, walk to the front of the house, and set off down the road.

I was chilled to the bone, trembling and shaking. As I walked and stumbled I was telling myself that I had had her so often and so well in that same bed, and in the motor car and on the ground by the Thompson. But all the time I knew that tonight he would be having her. That he could this night, and every night after if he choose, have her. And he could, if he chose, fall asleep with his hand between her thighs, as I used to fall asleep with her. Every night from now on.

And in the morning he would walk the streets and visit neighbours with her. He would sit beside her in the car. In front of others he would ask her opinion, and discuss his plans and hopes with her, in the open, acknowledged; in these ways I had never had her, never known her, and never would.

I thought of that, and thought how pathetic I was. What a small, bitter, thwarted animal, clutching at my little triumphs, relishing my little hatreds. What a child I was. I looked up from the road. Over the town the moon, now so much less than half full, had risen.

I was on the bench in the darkness at the rail station. Fifty or sixty yards away four CPR workmen stood around outside their bunkhouse, lit up by the carbide lamp overhead, smoking and talking and doing the same thing as myself: watching the arrivals at the Hotel a hundred yards away.

I had been there since seven o'clock. Several times women in twos and threes, in evening dress and long gloves, had come walking stiff and upright out of the dark dirt streets, and stepped onto the porch. A couple of democrats had come up and stopped along the side of the Hotel and older, quieter women with their older and quieter-again husbands had got down and gone inside. Brisk young men, a few, strangers to me, had stepped up and entered, the brittle sounds of their talking coming over the still air. But she hadn't come; not her, nor her husband.

I heard steps behind me, but I didn't look around and no one spoke for a while.

'Can't stand those moths around the lamp. So early in the summer and moths everywhere. And that gallump Albert swatting at them.'

'Hello Terry.'

'Evening, Jack. Are you going over?'

'No.'

'Lovely suit you have on.'

Two women came along the street and stopped and looked at each other, until one, the younger, put her hand to the small of the back of the other and together they silently stepped up onto the porch and went forward and inside.

'Mrs Collingwood and Mrs Trip,' said Terry. 'The ladies. The ladies who are fond of each other.'

Inside the Hotel the band, piano, violin, clarinet, played My Chocolate Soldier Sammy Boy.

'If I was you I'd go over there.'

'Yes.'

'Catchy tune, that,' said Terry. 'New, too. Have you been invited?'

'Yes.'

'Then I'd be over there. There would be lots of drinks over there, I bet yah. There would be at a welcome home do.' I sat there thinking about over there. 'You haven't been to any of the others? There's little mention of the Prohibition, I hear.' I took a half bottle of bourbon out of my jacket pocket. It was almost empty. I held it out to Terry. He smiled and didn't take it. 'I thought so.'

A Chinese waiter came come out and stared across as if he could see us, which I doubted, and looked up at the sky and went inside again.

'Poor George. His arm's sore pouring them drinks,' said Terry. He came around and sat on the bench beside me. Old Willie in his Sunday suit came along the street and loitered on the Hotel porch. He fiddled with his tie. He paced about, dense white hair standing out against the darkness under the porch. Sometimes he stood looking in the window at whatever was inside.

'You could go and join them posh folks. You and Willie.' The piano, violin and clarinet played Keep the Home Fires Burning. 'You could go and see the gents and their missuses on this lovely social occasion.'

A young man, again in evening dress, distinctive with his limp, came closer from the dark street and into the light of the porch and entered the hotel. 'Wee Jameson,' said Terry. 'You'd know him coming a mile away with that peg leg of his. He'll never get a woman.' A few minutes after that my landlady Mrs Hudson, even her in a smart dark dress and stole, followed him. The piano, violin and clarinet played Over There. There was a low rumble in the distance, then clanking, the sound of the evening transcontinental freight from the east heading for the end of the line in far-off Vancouver.

'Don't you have something to do, Terry? Some train business?'

'This one just rattles through.'

And then over the sound of the far-off train was the burble of a motor car, the dim headlamps coming out of the blackness of the streets from the end of town. It came closer and it was the Gray-Dort. It pulled up at the Hotel porch and I looked at it and at Sarah behind the wheel, wearing something pale and with a dark stole over her shoulders. I could imagine her shoulders under that stole, the few freckles, the little earlobes in which no doubt she had hung a pair of those earrings I had grown used to seeing scattered about her dressing table. Her hair was up and there was the back of her neck. Once I used to kiss it. The scent of her, the warmth of her skin, the feel of her sweat when we would come in out of the sun and stand in the shadows of the house and I would put my tongue to her neck and taste her.

And beside her the man who was her husband. I formed the words on my lips. Her husband. With Edward. I hated myself. For my weakness. For being this sick with longing.

There was another man in the back of the car, like her husband in evening dress, his hair thick and unruly, and as Sarah turned off the engine he was already climbing down onto the roadway. I watched him, this stranger, who would not stay a stranger. Terry had a hand out, pointing.

'That would be him,' he said. 'The hero.' I thought he meant Edward, but later I thought he meant the other. I couldn't tell if he was sincere. Sarah descended, and Edward, and they stood there, the three of them, Edward with his left arm stiff by his side, her pale in the gaslight, the stranger the smallest of the three. An old lover of Sarah's? Her new lover? So soon, a new lover? There was madness in that and I knew it even as the words formed, these bad angel's thoughts, but I formed them anyway and held them there: Sarah's new lover. The man went to the front of the Gray-Dort, his over-large head illuminated by each light in turn as he bent to extinguish the lamps. Above the regular clank and rattle of the approaching train I could hear him chattering back to Sarah, or imagined I could, and see his quick movements.

'Harry Garrard, the man who out Indians the Indian, out Eskimos the Eskimo. Mr Underhill's cousin.' Terry's finger rose again. 'He came in on the two fifteen today. Mrs Underhill was down picking him up. The first time I've seen her since she was here to get her husband home on Monday. Whatever they've been spending their time doing since I've no idea.'

Her husband held out his good arm to Sarah. This man, this weakened stick, was offering to support her. She took the arm. She was touching him. Then she stopped. Her head went down as she spoke to Willie on a chair on the porch near the door. Willie got to his feet, said something to Sarah. Her hand went out to his arm, then she moved off again into the Hotel, her husband on one side, Willie on the other, Harry Garrard walking behind. They were all gone and there was only the dark empty motor car on the street.

The long freight train was behind me, five, six yards away, wagon after wagon clanking and rattling over the points, the bell clanging, clanging. I turned on the seat, away from the Hotel. By the starlight I counted the wagons heading to the coast. There was a flare beside me as Terry struck a match, the quick smell of the tobacco from a cigarette. Seventy-three wagons. When the last wagon, with the last clank, the last rattle, the last clang had gone, the night was silent again, for the rail men at the cabins had gone too, their carbide lamp extinguished, and all was dark, except for the glow from the Hotel at the far end of the street, and from Terry's cigarette beside me.

I could hurry across there and be with Sarah. If I crossed that ground, crossed that road, passed her car and stepped up, I would see her across a well-lit room, moving, breathing, talking. I could go to her and seize her hands. My Sarah, no longer my Sarah. I could not seize her hands. In that room or anywhere public I could never have seized her hands.

'A lovely woman that Mrs Underhill. See her taking old Willie under her wing there?' The piano, violin, clarinet were playing Sister Susie's Sewing Shirts for Soldiers. 'Wee Jameson will be dancing with her.' I got to my feet and took a step away from the bench. 'Don't stint yourself on the drinks, boss.'

'I'll bring you out some, Terry. I'll bring you out some in my pocket. I'll pour it in. Pockets full of booze. Just you sit here and I'll be right back with the pockets and pockets full of booze.'

I crossed the uneven open ground and onto the roadway, and kept going, walking quickly as if I might change my mind, and to the door. The smell of roast meat was coming out on warm air, the smell of whiskeys and brandies, of cigars, the perfumes of ladies. The smells of the limping young and tottering old men, and of the young single women and the married women and the widows.

The band had stopped playing. Ahead of me a Chinese servant carried a tray of glasses towards the lights and sounds of the dining room. I followed him, and stopped at one side of the doorway. A few paces inside the room, standing, hands clasped, watching, with that tight limited smile, Miss Weir. A bar was open, with a Chinese bartender. Between the cream walls and the dark wood beams a scattering of women and a dozen older men like Major Sidgwick sitting at the square tables. Younger men stood about, drinks in hand, on the thick flower-patterned carpets. She, Sarah, with her husband and Harry Garrard at a table close to the big red-brick fireplace.

I moved away from the doorpost into the room. 'Good evening, Mr Butler.' Eleanor Weir. Black armband still in place, but the portrait of her brother no longer on the wall. Gordon, though, still in France. 'Welcome to our club.' I walked past her to the bar.

'George.' The young Chinaman polished a tumbler. He nodded and didn't smile. 'What's the form, George? Are drinks free?'

'You member?'

'How do I join your lovely club, George? How do I join?'

'Price of first drink.'

I put a dollar on the bar. Halfway along the bar Willie stood with a whiskey, looking down at the little drinks mat, at his hands. I walked down to stand beside him. The bartender filled the tumbler to the brim with whiskey and put the cloth over his shoulder and carried the tumbler to the far end of the bar. 'You order dinner?' he said in passing. I shook my head. A man I hadn't seen before, with a scarred face, a stump where his left hand should be, waited at the far end of the bar, holding an empty whiskey glass in his good right hand. He put the empty glass down, picked up the full glass. No money changed hands. I turned my back on the bar and looked across the room.

Sarah was bent towards Harry Garrard. A pin in her hair, some coloured thing, maybe a gift brought from Europe. She seemed paler. The electric light. Or maybe I miss-remembered. Nine days. I couldn't forget in nine days. Harry Garrard was doing the talking, his hands moving over the tablecloth. He picked up a tumbler, moved it next to a small dish of nuts, ran a finger across the table and wove it between the glass and the dish. Beside me Willie watched this as well. Harry Garrard's hand rose and waved to describe direction, of wind or snow or herds of caribou or the flow of rivers. Only he and Sarah knew, for Edward was leaning back, talking to Major Sidgwick at the next table. The Major's blind eyes moved around, over the fireplace, over Edward's face, over his shoulder and stayed there, as if he too was watching Sarah and her guest. Or listening. His head turned aside, presenting an ear.

I could hear somebody talking to the scarred man behind me.

'So we got all these berries and crushed them up and set to work and we made all this drink out them. Then I thought: we don't really know what these berries are or what might be in them. We'd better look them up. So while the alcohol matured I got a book and identified them and read all about 'em. They contain cyanide, the book said. Cyanide, I said. Well! Maybe we'd better not drink this after all…'

These ridiculous clown Englishmen.

'What do you make of it, Willie?' Leaning over Mrs Hudson and talking to Jameson was a pretty young woman of about nineteen in a shining blue dress, long pearls hanging from her neck, her blonde hair cut in a bob.

'Miss Gore Ward,' he said. 'Mrs Scott's younger sister. I've been driving her about.' He drained his whiskey. 'It was Mrs Underhill asked me here. I don't like it.'

'Why's that?'

'I'm like a pig in a parlour.'

'What the hell do they know?'

'And the hired help treat you like horse shit on a shoe.'

'George,' I called. 'My whiskey. My glass of whiskey.' He came towards me, and picked up a bottle. 'Black Bush.' He put down the bottle, picked up another bottle and poured. 'As full as that one.' I pointed down the bar to the man with the stump of an arm. George poured again. I pushed the glass of Black Bush over to Willie. 'And another one. One for me. As big as that one.' George poured again. I drained it. 'Another one.'

'You'll have to pay again, sir.' I looked back into the un-smiling face.

'Pour me another one.'

'I say. No need to shout.' The ridiculous voice again. I spun round. Somebody, some ex-soldier toff I didn't know, in evening dress.

'Mind your own god damned business.'

'I say…'

'Don't say. Shut the hell up.'

'You're insulting my fellow officer.' The man with the stump of an arm. His scarred face was livid. 'I've looked for-ward to this night. To stand in my little town again.' His good hand was tightening on the empty whiskey glass. 'You're not going to spoil it.' I reached over and plucked the bottle of Black Bush out of George's hand, took a pull out of it, and grasped it by the neck. I swung back. Whiskey spilled across the floor. The man stepped in closer.

'Lieutenant Fielder. And Monty, you idiot.' A woman's voice. Not Sarah's. 'Mr Butler. It is you, isn't it? I'd thought I wasn't going to meet you.' I looked into her face. The young woman with the blonde bob, the blue dress, the long string of fake pearls.

'Heroes, all of them. English bloody English heroes.'

'Many were, Mr Butler. Both these chaps, I'm very sure. Why don't you come and sit with me?'

'How sweet. How bloody bloody sweet and civil and sweet.'

'Absolutely.' She held up a glass of something with fruit in it. 'These are full of goodness. Or I could get you some cof-fee, Mr Butler. Why don't you put the bottle down?' I stood there and looked at her. She had nothing to do with this. In her blue shining dress and her blonde bob and her pearls and her youth. I put the bottle down.

'I apologise.'

'That's not a bad idea. Why don't you apologise to Lieutenant Fielder and Captain Montgomery too? And George here?'

'We all have our moments.' The ridiculous voice. I had my back to them. I kept it like that.

'He's not worth it,' said Lieutenant Fielder.

'Perhaps not,' said the other.

'So what kept you away until now, Mr Butler?'

'I was counting rail wagons.'

'I beg your pardon?' Her brow furrowed and then cleared again. 'You are being Irish.'

'I am being silly, Miss Gore Ward.'

'You are certainly being that. And you know my name.'

'As you know mine.'

Miss Gore Ward leant closer to speak into my ear. 'Where is everybody else tonight, Mr Butler? I thought there would be more?'

Edward was lighting a cigarette. He put his hand on Sarah's shoulder, telling her something. Sarah was looking up at him as he spoke. She had a little smile. There was a flowered scent from the woman beside me, the first time I was aware of it. How good that was in this ugly and bitter little room.

'Yes, Miss Gore Ward. Oh yes, yes, yes.'

'Do you want to stay here? Because I think I've had enough of this just now. Enough of other things too.' She put her glass on the bar. 'I'm going outside for a cigarette. Why don't you come with me? Get some fresh air.'

'We can leave together. Yes. See you, Willie.' I took her by the arm and we walked out together but when I paused at the door and looked back Sarah still had eyes only for her husband.

CHAPTER TEN

HARRY WAS WAKING UP. He seemed a little better; strong enough anyway to fuss.

'The bones,' he said. 'That's why I have cramps. We are bound up by bone meal and eating the hides hair and all.' His voice rose, calling. 'Can't you see it? I need an enema. We all need enemas. Edward.'

Edward was coming awake.

'How would I do that, Harry?'

'You are a good pal, Edward. The rubber tube for siphoning lamp oil. That would do. The funnel. Grease. And warm water.'

When I saw Edward get out of his bunk and begin to poke at the ashes of the stove I rose and put on the capote and took myself outside on the crutch, trailing the .303 with me. I went down to the ice of the river, and managed to get upstream for nearly a hundred yards. The rise of a few degrees, the stillness, the clear sky, made a difference. If we had even a little food, I thought, even a little... I rested on an isolated spruce stump, cut when we had strength in the autumn. I bent forward, the rifle in my lap, exhausted from getting this far. I inhaled, the air cutting my throat. I held the breath, warmed it, exhaled. Again.

There was the steam of a kitchen on a damp day. Condensation on the window pane. I could feel the warmth of the black range. A cloth hung drying on a line above the range, a blue and white striped kitchen cloth. There was a taste in my mouth: apple tart. Apple tart with a little cinnamon, like those my mother baked every October. The darkness of the pastry above, the paleness as it peeled back. The firmness of the apple, the crunch and sweetness of the sugar, the sticky feel on my tongue and lips. I knew I was asleep, but wanted to stay in that state, and then the warmth and food and its smells all drifted away, and I knew I was sitting on a stump by the Thelon River with my eyes closed, and near death.

I opened my eyes and a wolverine was ten or twelve feet away. It had been creeping towards me, knowing my state as well as myself. Hoping, I expect, as we poor bare, forked animals in the cabin hoped, for food to fall to it. I raised the rifle in my arms, the butt against my chest, the barrel circling, circling, and when I thought it was in the direction of the motionless sharp face I pulled the trigger. The recoil knocked me off the stump, and I lay there, hoping the wolverine would not be at my throat, for I had no more strength to pull the bolt back and raise the rifle again. But nothing happened, and when I sat up the wolverine was dead in the snow, a hole in the side of its head. Blood I could have drunk had run away into an already stiffening puddle, and Edward, having heard the shot, was coming laboriously towards me, a knife in his hand.

I lay on the bunk while Edward fried the meat.

'Harry,' he would say. 'Harry... we have food. Smell that. Good meat. Any minute now.' And when the first strips were fried he chopped them and carried them to Harry, who put a little in his mouth and waved the rest away. 'I'll keep yours for later, Harry,' said Edward, and we ate, finding we could only swallow a little ourselves, ravenous though we were.

Harry slept and Edward wrote in his notebook again. While they slept and wrote I watched over the meat in the pan on the table, drifting in and out of awareness, but a share of that meat was mine and, able to eat it or not, I'd have killed anybody who tried to take it from me.

Monday, 19th May 1919

I had written nothing in my journal for weeks, but that was an easy date to remember, for it was Victoria Day. I had slept late and walked in the town in the empty streets. They would be at Twin Lakes. Her and Edward and Hector. All their friends, any who were still here. Who else had this hatred of the end of the War? Who else had so much hatred? I think I flattered myself. I was human and my hatred was probably not that special, not that unique, not, possibly, all that strong. But when I hadn't her it seemed it was all I had.

Not everyone had stayed all day at Twin Lakes. For now on this warm fine late afternoon Helen Gore Ward was walking beside me along River Road. The road was hard and not yet dusty and the small trees in the orchards either side had young soft leaves fully open, and the short-lived pink and white blossom falling in drifts. The earth in one orchard had been dug by some returned hero and filled with seed potatoes in rows between the trees. The earth had not been heaped up enough, and in the dry and disturbing winds to come the potatoes would be left bare under the hot sun and shrivel. I would let them. On the hills far away across the Thompson a scattering of tiny flowers had come out, pink and yellow and blue against the brown of the earth. There was green on the flat benches that was leathery bunch grass, or other wiry tough shrubs with their spines, their barbs, their toxic leaves, but which in the distance gave a soft look to this place that would not return until next spring.

I'd come to Footner on a day not that different to this, and all I had seen was dryness and barrenness, and I'd stayed anyway. I'd stayed through the short rest of that spring and into the summer, when the earth became bald and hot all the time and dust blew from field to field and into the Thompson. I'd stayed on into a hard winter where the wind and snows came down from the Barrens in the north and the Rockies to the east and a spade wouldn't turn in the earth. I'd stayed for Sarah. But what was I staying for now?

'Or if I could get the gasoline, enough gas to just get there and back, we could go tomorrow and take in a flicker in Cache Creek,' she was saying. 'They tried to keep gin from us, and now there's hardly any gasoline.' I was looking at the side of her face, at that smooth cheek, where the blonde bob of her hair swung across beneath a cloche hat, and trying to tell myself I found her attractive, that I enjoyed her company, that very soon I would be getting beyond chit chat about the flowers coming on the apple trees and the flickers in Cache Creek and onto standing her behind one of these small apple trees and kissing her.

'I will be at work tomorrow. That thing.'

'Oh that,' she said. She wore a dress with little silver beads on it, a whole silver-coloured dress, and there was a pale silk scarf hanging from her neck, and it all moved in the sunlight as she moved. I wore my suit. Edward's suit.

'Sure. That.' The warm smell of horticultural oil was in the air. I put my hand up as if I could feel it, my fingers moving. The memory that was in it had me sick and sad and tired. I had no interest in kissing her.

'Well, that is why you are here. Work.'

'Yes.'

She turned quickly as if to see what I looked like. 'You know that never made sense.' We kept walking. 'It doesn't make sense,' she said again when I said nothing.

'Not everything has to make sense.'

'Oh? I was brought up to believe things probably did make sense, if only we understood them.'

'But you don't believe that now, do you?'

'Certainly not.' She shook her head, and her hair swung forward from beneath her cloche hat. 'Nobody believes that now.' Her raised hand held a cigarette and she drew on it and puffed the smoke out into the still air in front of her. 'I am going to get a job. I am. I could write for a newspaper.' Close to her there was her flowered scent, one I thought of as lilies. It was a good scent and expensive and mixed with the cigarette smoke and suited her. 'Not near here of course.' She was looking around her. 'Not anywhere here.' She flung the half-smoked cigarette into the green bunch grass at the side of the road. 'I'm a big city girl. I could never stay in the sticks for long. Are you a big city boy?' She had asked before where I was from, and I had told her of Richhill, and a little about what it was like. What it might be like.

'A small town boy.'

'A small town in Ireland. I see it. One street. People sitting out on it in the evenings. Everybody knowing everything about everybody else.'

'That's the place.'

She was looking down at her shoes as she walked. They were little pale slippers, scratched from the stones and the earth.

'Why so abrupt? Have I annoyed you? Anyway. Had I been older I would have insisted on being a nurse in the War.' Her mouth was tighter now. She shook her head. 'Too late now for that one.'

'There's still time. People are always selfish and sick and dying. Doing it in droves at this very moment, I hear.'

She walked on, mouth a little open, silent. Then she swung around.

'Would you like me to go away? I thought you were starting to like me?' She was making a little mouth shape, telling me I hadn't shocked her by how I spoke. I watched her, the face moving from quietness to the little pout and now on to a smile. Then that was gone. How easily she did these things, these changes, like a child. She was looking ahead again, and her head rose. 'I'll get my way,' she said.

We had passed the last of the orchards. The land on our left lay roughly fenced and no cultivation had begun. On our right was the drop to the benches two hundred feet below, and the river below that again, and hanging out over the river the water pipe from the north side.

'What did you do on your days off before I came here?' she said.

'Counted train wagons.'

'Silly man. And all these young abandoned women.'

I did like her. Who else was there here who wouldn't take offence at my linking dying with selfishness? Who else would have made a joke about young abandoned women? Her, that other, whom I had thought of instantly at the smell of the horticultural oil.

She began to hum something as she walked. Her voice rose and fell and her chin rose with the higher notes. She looked round at me and saw me watching her and smiled and kept on humming. Suddenly she took my arm and started to run, but I didn't go with her. She let go and ran a few steps and looked back at me with her eyes wide, and stopped humming and laughed. She was panting, not from exertion, but alive and happy.

I held up a finger. 'Old Dog Trey?'

'Puccini.' She punched my arm. 'It was Pu...' punch 'cci...' punch 'ni,' punch.

'You look very pretty when you're punching me.'

'Are you a man or what, to let me?'

We walked on. We were still on the heights and the land open all around us, not even the rough fences, and the air still and the sun pleasant.

'So: have you any sources of gasoline?' she said. 'Anybody you know, maybe, who has some and isn't using it much?' What did she know? I waited but her face was still turned away from me. 'You know I'm leaving next week?'

We went on over the heights until the land fell away in front of us and there was the bend of the Thompson in the distance in the bright clear air, and the Government Bridge, and between us and the bridge a man walking. Walking quickly up the slope towards us, a rapid short-legged walk, and he had no hat on and his head of thick black hair was moving rhythmically, bobbing with the force of his walk on the rough road.

'Our visitor,' she said. 'Our guest. Mr Charlie Chaplin. All he needs is the little cane.'

'Mr Explorer.'

'Mr who doesn't wash quite as much as he should, and who might lose that habit of taking his teeth out at odd moments. Have you been introduced yet?' I was studying this small man. 'But he is extraordinary,' she said. We watched his little agitated walk. 'I've been insulting him while trying to be funny, but he is extraordinary.'

'Yes.'

'Yes, he is.' She said it firmly. 'He has lived a life like no one else I know.'

'Yes.'

'He has.'

I breathed in her lily scent and we watched the man come closer and then he was thirty, twenty, paces away. He was dark skinned, with those white teeth, his legs bent like someone who had rickets as a child, his eyes under the black curls quick and guilty and sharp. We came to a stop and then he was an arm's length away. All the last part of his approach those eyes were on me, then as he stopped they swung away.

'Miss Gore Ward,' he said. He stood there, his face a little flushed, panting, which surprised me. He was about forty, maybe older. He wore a good suit of a heavy dark woollen cloth and a white shirt and a red tie in a broad knot, and carried a straw boater in his hand and he flapped his face with the boater. 'Miss Gore Ward.'

'Mr Garrard.'

He put the boater on his head and pushed some of his hair under it. 'I beg your pardon.' His eyes were looking somewhere past her and then darting back to her and then away again.

'You are not enjoying the holiday at Twin Lakes?' she asked him. She was tugging at the pale silk scarf around her neck and curling an end of it around a finger. 'May I ask: did you walk far, Mr Garrard?'

'The Ashcroft road and back.' He nodded.

'I'm told lots of people used to like to ride out over the ranges. I'm afraid we don't have very many places to walk here. There is indeed nothing but the bare main road this way.' His head nodded once more. 'If I had more gasoline I wouldn't be walking here myself.' His eyes came to her face and flicked away again. 'Though I expect you are used to walks a lot longer than that.'

'Yes,' he said. 'I expect so.'

'Very arduous walks and dog sledge journeys and, oh who knows what. Were you in training just now?'

'No. No.' He was moving his feet around on the roadway as if he wanted to be off again. Feet in scuffed and dirty black boots. A lace dangled. He had got his breathing under control. His face was calming too. On it were the lines that age and hard living had put, a deep line either side of a large and sharp nose. 'It's somewhat hot for me.' He said it to her but then glanced at me. How startlingly pale blue those eyes were. 'I'm not used to this.'

'Why, Mr Garrard, this is like a spring day in Hertfordshire.'

'I am used to something different.' While he had the wild black hair and bent legs and battered boots and the habits with his teeth he spoke in that same English public school voice of Footner.

'Of course Mr Garrard.' She left her scarf alone. 'Of course.'

He took off the straw boater once more and started to walk away and then turned and called back, 'I beg your pardon. It has been lovely to meet you again, Miss Gore Ward,' and kept going in that abrupt short-legged walk of his. The straw boater was waving in his hand, the black hair bobbing.

We watched him go and then turned to each other, and she said, 'What do you make of that?'

'What do you make of it?'

'An eccentric but brave man living the life he loves in the places he loves. I admire him for it.' She waited and I didn't either agree or disagree. 'A suit from Savile Row and boots from Dawson City. I think he has signs of greatness.'

'Yes. Let's go on.' At Twin Lakes she was picking up plates, he was playing cricket. They were smiling, at everyone, at each other. He would put his arm around her. She would let him.

'Don't you think so?' Then when I said nothing, 'Are you jealous?' She raised her right hand and waved it with two fingers up as if it should contain a cigarette.

'That I don't have signs of greatness?' Did she think of last year? Did she think of me?

'No. That I clearly admire this older man,' she said. 'Have you any cigarettes? I have nothing with me.'

'Let's forget Harry Garrard.'

She held up her empty hands. 'No, of course you don't have a cigarette. You are a pure man with no vices. As I am a pure girl with no vices. Except smoking and drinking gin when I get it and letting men kiss me sometimes. Do you think that's shocking?'

But I had had enough of playful things.

Yet we walked on down to the Government Bridge, and there we threw stones in the Thompson like children might, and watched a gopher dart in and out of a hole at the edge of the bridge. All the time I was thinking of that other, but we went down a little slope on the bank and under the bridge, and there Helen Gore Ward stood with her back against an iron stanchion and I made myself kiss her for a long time.

There had been a time when I had been truly happy and, in the very moment, known it.

An autumn day, lying out along that water pipe where it crossed the Thompson, tightening bolts on one of the hawsers, to haul the pipe up high above the river before the torrents of winter and the floods of spring swept it away.

I had stopped working, the big spanner in one hand, holding onto the hawser with the other. I was thinking of Sarah. I remember looking at the flakes of rust on the head of the bolt three or four inches in front of me. The speckles of dark iron among the coppery red. And after looking at that bolt and the red speckles for an age, I looked down past the bolt and hawser and into the river tearing, glittering, past below, and I felt the greatest surge of happiness, of good luck, of contentment, I have ever known. My Sarah. I had wanted her, and this autumn, this day, this instant, she was mine. My epiphany, above the waters of the Thompson, was that at no time in my life would I ever be happier again than I was at that moment.

Then I forgot about it, until now.

The sun not yet hot, no wind, the sky cloudless. That, anyway, is how I remember it: a perfect and beautiful early summer day. In the yard of the Dunae house, sawing planks of wood to length for the flume, trying to get some uniformity into that ramshackle thing. As if I cared. It was her who kept me here, and him, who would in a moment approach and ask me to call at his house that evening. Hatred shackling me as much as love ever did.

I heard the borrowed Gray-Dort come bumping towards me. I glanced up—what cvb was I looking for, what was I hoping?—saw the two people in it, and bent and pushed the saw through the wood again. Then came the familiar grind of brakes, and the engine idling. After a moment I heard the footsteps in the yard behind me.

'Mr Butler?' I put down the saw and turned. There he was: in a tan suit, a white shirt, a brown tie. His trousers stopped above long stockings, a wide felt hat on his head. He had a slight smile below the clipped moustache in that thin, sunken face, left arm straight by his side, and he was holding out his other hand. 'Mr Butler. I think I should introduce myself.' As if. As if I would not know. 'Edward Underhill.' I looked at the outstretched hand, and moved my own hand away. He could imagine it was dirty, or that he was being snubbed, or whatever he liked. The little wispy smile in the thin face stayed. How unimportant my handshake was to him. Something else, petty, that I could hate him for. 'I hear from so many people you have been doing wonders in our manpower shortage.' I couldn't help but smile at the English voice saying that. I saw his own smile broaden, pleased, thinking I was friendly towards him. I had done wonders in the manpower shortage.

'Well, Captain Underhill.' I could play this role. 'That's nice to hear. I hope Mrs Underhill thinks so too. But now of course you are home you will be performing those tasks yourself.' How could even he not see through this? I glanced over his shoulder. Sarah, behind the wheel, in her white gloves and straw boater, looking straight ahead. Yet these things would only hurt him if he was someone attuned to deviousness. He wouldn't see them because he was not like that. Because he was not me. The only person I was hurting was myself.

'Call me Edward. Please. I was stopping to ask if you'd like to come up to the house sometime. Tonight would be a good time.' His smile seemed to have hardened. 'Our guest Mr Garrard has expressed an interest in meeting you.' The smile tightened further. As if there was a physical pain and not wanting to betray it. 'And we'd like to have you as well.' The smile was slowly widening again.

I was watching that expression, the smile that tightened and slackened. His silly introduction of himself. I had done wonders. A fool who deserved to be a cuckold. I would never come to his house. Never again.

'What do you make of Footner, Captain Underhill, after all your time away?' Was he hoping for cricket soon? A hunt?

Tennis? Some golf? I ached to goad him. 'What do you think of its prospects?' I watched the curve of his mouth. The smile remained. His head shook.

'It's the aftermath of the War, old boy. Of course it is. Things will pick up again soon. You'll see. Wait till all the chaps get themselves sorted out. Things have to settle. Well, I must be off. About eight. Good day.' And he turned, hurrying away, to get into the Gray-Dort. Taking it for granted I would come. Then he turned in his seat and called out, 'You will come, won't you?' As the motor car moved off he waved. Sarah looked straight ahead, and at the last minute turned, blank-faced, towards me, and then looked forward again.

I watched her now, as I had before, go away from me towards town, and I remembered how on that other day I, not the man beside her, had been the naïve and fooled one.

CHAPTER ELEVEN

THE NEXT DAY the small pieces of meat that Edward put into
Harry's mouth dribbled out again uneaten. Harry didn't
leave his bunk, and Edward would give him enemas with hot
water and wolverine grease from the rubber tube, to little im-
provement that I could see.

While Harry lay deeply asleep, Edward, beside his bunk,
began to talk to me over his shoulder.

'At Aubers, there was a dead man, completely naked.
Couldn't see a mark on him. Strangest thing. We put an old
shirt on him and put him in the grave. Rankin straightened
out his legs. Saying, You'll be cold tonight. But kindly.' A
little silence fell, apart from the deep breathing of Harry. 'Is
that why I think of it?'

He turned away from Harry. He looked into my face. His
hand came out as if to touch mine but then paused in front
of me.

'This hand, on all those dead. This. Taking off their discs.
Putting it into their pockets. Looking for papers. After
months, some of them. At Poziers. Ancre Heights. Lys. The
things this hand has touched. Rags of men.' He leant forward
until his face was close to mine, speaking slowly, tiredly.
'Legs, arms, sticking out, our men. Or Germans. Does it matter? We'd shake a hand going past. How do you do, we'd
say.' His hand rose and fell, shaking those dead hands.
'Splendid weather we're having. I shook their hands.'

His own hand was lowered, and he sat for a little. Then,
'Second Lieutenant Shearman hanging on the wire. How he
got bloated. Old Jimmy's putting on weight, we'd say. Then
he burst open. Old Jimmy's lost weight. Looking better, we'd
say. I introduced him so the relief would joke too.' The voice

had slowed further. 'My head is full of these things.' His tongue came out to his dark lips, and licked them, and he went on. 'Other things too. We got grenades into a German machine gun post.' These words came slowest of all. 'They were lying there. An officer and three men. All alive. Their hands up. *Meine Frau... meine armen Kinder.* I shot them in the face, one after another. All of them. With my Webley. Emptied it.' He stopped. When he spoke again I could hardly hear him. 'How was I to tell Sarah that?'

I looked back into his face. Then I couldn't any more, and I turned away and fiddled with the bones on the table.

For two more days and nights Harry drifted in and out of consciousness. I saw him alive about ten thirty on the evening of April 15th, when I helped Edward turn him in his filthy bunk. His lips were moving a little, and his eyes were open, but there was no indication he was making sense of anything. When I woke in the morning Edward was sitting on the tin trunk beside him and holding his hand. Edward's head was down, and I thought he was asleep, but when I moved the blankets he looked up.

'Harry's gone,' he said. 'It was about a quarter to seven.'

My first thought was that whatever we found to eat would be divided two ways now instead of three.

Then I made myself rise. I lit the fire, and all the time Edward sat on holding the dead man's hand. I made tea, and put sugar in it and brought Edward a cup. There was Harry's face above the blankets, the wild beard, the tangled curly hair, which Edward had tidied back, his dirty and sunken skin, with its darker scabs and sores, the blisters, the patches of dead whiteness from frostbite, his toothless mouth. His eyes were only partly closed, and the red rims still showed. Edward let go of Harry's hand, and drank his tea, all the time trembling.

'Lie down. Let yourself sleep for a while.'

'You are a good pal,' he said. He was taking deeper breaths.

'I'll cut more wood. I'm feeling strong today. I'll get out with the rifle.'

'Yes,' said Edward. 'What would I do without you?' At that he began to sob, shaking. 'We have to pull together.' He went to put the cup on the floor, and it toppled over. He began to apologise.

'Ssssh. Lie down.' I grasped his shoulders and helped him as far as his bunk, and there he lay, the thick red tartan blanket on top of all the other bedclothes. He closed his eyes and was still, but I had no way of knowing if he was asleep or not. After I had stoked up the fire I looked at him again. He had turned his face to the cabin wall, and seemed to be sleeping deeply.

I went back to Harry's bunk, and looked down at the litter of bones and chewed sinew on his blankets, the small bulge of the man beneath. The red-rimmed eyes troubled me most. As long as I could see them I had some suspicion he was still alive. Maybe not as we had known him, but alive. I thought if I did not close his eyes I would dream of him, and I dreaded dreaming of him. I put my fingers on his eyelids. How cold they were. I pushed them down, but they had already become fixed. I pushed again, and felt the give of the eye underneath, but the eyelids did not close and the red rims were still there.

On impulse I reached down under the blankets and put my hand on his jacket over his heart. Was I checking for a last beat? All I found was coldness and stillness. He was as dead as he was ever going to be.

The bird enters, darts through the refectory, and returns to the night. Maybe I made a mistake. Maybe I should have chosen to begin here instead, at this moment in my flash of light. It was, after all, the beginning of the end.

In the clear cold night air I walked towards that house on the bench. Of course I was going. I came over the brow of the hill, the land falling away, and there were the stars, as if more than ever, and there was the silver river, and there was the house, everything so still but the column of smoke from the chimney, long and straight and rising through the stars.

And in that house, around the fire, would be Mr Edward Underhill, recently of the Front, of the Mauretania, and Harry Garrard, and her. There would be warmth. A meal ready, the smells of meat and thyme or sage in the rooms. The smell of whiskey—no, whisky. Edward drank Glenfiddich. Harry Garrard and Edward smoking Edward's Three Castles cigarettes. Her drinking a Gordon's and tonic. She may have played something on the piano, and laughed. They would be deep in conversation now, bantering. Always her laughing. And I would arrive. I would walk up to the door and knock and Edward would open it and I would say 'Good evening. Nice of you and Mrs Underhill and Mr Garrard to ask me along,' and go in.

I kept walking over the rise and down, for if I hesitated I might turn back. Light shone out from the parlour windows. The tall brass lamp on the desk would be lit, and the green-shaded lamp on the bookcase. I went not to the door facing out into the yard, the one I had used so often, but up the three steps to the front door, the one that opened directly into the parlour, and stopped. I listened. The sounds of low conversation inside. I knocked twice, strongly, before I could turn away. A break in the chatter, footsteps across the rugs and wooden floor. The turning of the door knob.

Of course it was her. I stood there saying nothing, trying to read her, hunting for signs... of what? Worry. That was what I saw there. Worry no doubt that I would be foolish and say something I shouldn't. Give the game away. Not be a decent chap.

'Mr Butler. Come in. We have been hoping you would make it.' She stepped away from the door and turned aside and I could not see her expression any more. 'Mr Butler,' she called into the parlour, needlessly. There was a smell of cooking meat and herbs, of whisky, of Three Castles cigarettes. There was a woody green scent too, something of citrus in it, a new scent, and it came from her. Her dress was some blue thing I hadn't seen before. She was changing, had changed, everything from what she had with me to what she would have with him. Over her shoulder I could see the two men in the parlour waiting for me. Hector on the floor between them, his tail wagging quickly when he saw me. I stepped past her, and walked ahead. I would speak first. I could always speak, and smile, and act, the useless, passable things.

'Good evening. Thank you so much for having me.'

The men, in the leather chairs either side of the fireplace. Edward in her chair, in a dark suit, sitting quietly, cigarette in hand, smiling softly. And the other, in tweeds, thick black hair tousled, grinning, blue eyes and his so-white teeth, a cup of black tea in his hand. The Earl Grey that Sarah disliked but which Edward preferred? And if Edward smiled more widely might I see his gold tooth far back on the right? How had that come up, her telling me of it one night in her bed? These little things and more I knew of him.

'Good evening, Mr Butler. I knew you would make it up here once again.' Not Edward but his visitor. While she walked past me and into the kitchen. Had there been a look?

177

Any sort of look? 'Edward and I have been sorting out the world after the War.' Gesturing vigorously with the hand that held his cup and saucer. 'You can join us in that. Putting the place to rights. What do you say?' I didn't like Harry Garrard, but he had an energy missing in Edward. If I slapped him he'd fight back.

There was a tray of drinks on the table beside her chair, Edward's chair, whisky, brandy, thick tumblers, where she would put down her book as I came into the room from the back, past the kitchen and the bedroom. And she would look up... It would always have been Edward's chair, but I hadn't known that. His legs stretched out over the heavy red rug. He flicked his cigarette into the silver horseshoe ashtray on the table. Ash fell to the rug. He was getting to his feet. His hand came out again and this time I shook it. Why not?

'A drink before dinner? What will you have?'

'No. No, nothing.' A gin and tonic on top of a book case further away, beside a cane chair we had never used.

'Are you sure?' A certain look. He had noticed me in the Hotel at his welcome home, then. She would be doing something with pots and pans, plates, in the kitchen. Those new blue sleeves pushed up.

'No.' To speak strongly, to confront him over some little thing. 'I seldom drink.' But what did it matter? What did any of it matter?

'Take a seat, please.' Edward picking up a cane chair, carrying it to the fire. Using both arms. 'Have my seat, near the drinks in case you change your mind.' I took the cane chair before he could sit there himself.

'No. I'm fine here.'

She came out of the kitchen and towards us and turned into the dining room. Those sleeves arranged again before she appeared. To arrange something else in there, around the heavy table, the heavy chairs. Light the candles on those stands. While we had always eaten in the kitchen. Or from a plate on our knee on the porch, looking out over the Thompson in the cooling air of the summer evenings.

'We have to think about the good that's come out of the War.' Harry Garrard. Persistent, intrusive Harry Garrard. 'Do you know there's more red on the maps now than ever before?'

'Harry, you do talk a bit of rot.' Edward lit another cigarette from the one he was smoking. Had he picked up that habit in Flanders?

'What do you say, Mr Butler?'

I nodded at Harry, being agreeable. Harry, who had spent the War years exploring and starving in the Barrens. 'Certainly. You've made a good point there.' Anything, to find a way to disagree with Edward. Sarah, in the dining room. Sarah, touching things. She would be listening to this. She wouldn't like Harry either.

'You leap around from subject to subject, Harry.' Edward's eyes were on the red rug at his feet.

'No. The one subject: the reputation of the British Empire, into which we seem to have arrived at the optimum moment. Risen even higher, thanks to the War.' His black hair bouncing, drinking from his cup of black tea. I could almost see his legs swing in the chair, this little effervescent annoying ball of a man. Edward raised a heavy tumbler and took a long drink from it.

'I think dinner is almost ready.'

I could face that dinner. Or I could leave now, plead I was ill, something. But I wanted to sit across from Sarah, watch her, listen to her, not for the pleasure in it, not that any more, but for the pain of it. As if I would eventually have enough and it would burn out and I would never be in that place again.

I went in after Harry, after Edward, to see where they would sit, so I could sit across from Sarah, but Edward steered me to a seat across from Harry. When Sarah came out of the kitchen there was only the place left beside me, and she put a tureen on the table and sat there, tugging the chair away from me an inch, two inches.

What did we eat? What was the soup? What I remember is Harry Garrard telling his tales of the North, of his hunting, of the fortunes to be made, of the hardships. Of how tough he was. Of how he could out Indian the Indian, out Eskimo the Eskimo, out walk, out run, out starve everyone. But it let me sit unmolested and think of the woman beside me, of what she might be thinking, of what she made of this life after what she had when I lived in the bunkhouse, lived in her kitchen and in her bed, when we had made love on the red rug where Edward had dropped his cigarette ash. When we had no guests in the evening but each other and it was enough.

'The candles were made of string and fox fat, all we had left. Our last poor old dog had a foot stinking of gangrene and finally I had to shoot him.'

'This perfume, Mrs Underhill.' I imagined she stiffened. 'I think it's new, isn't it?' She moved a spoon about in whatever dish of meat and onions she had served and didn't reply. 'I sure I've never smelt anything like it before.'

'What a man you are for noticing women's things.' Edward. 'I never know, never did know, if she'd got a new dress or not. Isn't that right, dear?' I turned and watched her, waiting for the response. She put the silver spoon down in the bowl and put her hands in her lap. 'What you smell there is a thing called Bois. Very new. I got it under the counter in

Paris.' He tapped the side of his nose and smiled as if he had done something very devious.

'We had about three tons of icy gravel for a roof. The props could have gone down at any minute, at one careless brush against them. Critchell was edgy. I was resigned. There was wood for one more decent fire, and no food whatsoever.'

As we ate some dish of fruit that Sarah brought in Harry began to put my name into his talk. Enough to make me wonder again why he had wanted me here.

'My proposal is this, Mr Butler: of course Footner will get back its feet, but right now, and I don't think Edward will mind my saying this, there is a need for immediate action. Fund-raising action. That's exactly what I'm proposing.'

'What, Mr Garrard? What are you proposing?'

'Trapping.'

I think I laughed. 'No.' Is that what he had wanted me here for, to ask me to go hunting with him? 'Never again.'

'We take a train to Edmonton. I've heaps of old pals in Edmonton. Then another train to Waterways. The Muskeg Express. We are still in civilisation there. Then we throw a canoe, which we've got in Edmonton and taken out on the train with us, into the Athabasca...'

'I'm finished with all that.' What else could I say? I didn't look at Sarah, surprised she had told him anything about me.

'We leave early.' Harry's finger wagged, and he bounced around in his seat. 'Edward has never canoed. So, gaining experience and toughness as we go, we travel up the Slave River to Great Slave Lake.'

'Edward? Mr Underhill is going with you?' The thin man beside me, with the twitchy smile, the arm that sometimes seemed to work and at others not? 'I think it's a great idea that you and Mr Underhill go, but as for me...'

'The white purity that lies ahead.' Harry Garrard's hand broadened, swept round in a flat curve. 'Cleanness. Endless miles, in every direction.'

'Harry…' Edward, playing with his knife. 'I've said to you. You weren't to ask Mr Butler this.'

'Well, that's the thing, old boy.' The same hand coming out towards me. 'Without a sturdy and experienced third man we can't go. And I hear you are that very chap, Mr Butler.'

'And you heard that from?'

'A CPR chap I was talking to. Told me all about you. Old Edward's well mended, but Mrs Underhill's not going to let him go off into the wilderness without a care. What if something happened to me? The old crock?' He laughed, confident of his health, his toughness, that he would out-live us all.

'Edward.' She leant towards him, making him look at her. 'You have to put this idea out of your head. It is nonsense.' Sarah, loud and certain. Saying the first thing other than comments on the food since she had shown me into the parlour. 'You are not fit. It would be the end of you.' I smiled at her, though I felt little like smiling. She had chosen Edward over me. Now he was proposing to leave her again.

'Darling…' Darling. 'Sarah.' He lit another cigarette. 'From what Harry says there is good money to be made from one winter in the North, one winter of trapping fox.' He drew on the cigarette and looked down at the table, at his plate with his mess of fruit on it. I could admire Edward, a little, then. In his state of health, just back after sheltering in a hole with death and the fear of death, offering to go away again, because he thought it was the thing he should do. I could also think it madness. 'But I don't think that Mr Butler is the man to go with us. Mr Butler's place is in Footner.'

The officer and gentleman didn't want the Irishman workman with him. The snob. Yet one more thing to hate him for. If he didn't want me then I might feel more like going.

'You get paid a quarter of the furs, Mr Butler. After dinner, a cup of tea, Mrs Underhill? A cup of black, maybe? Not wages, but a share of the fur that will be much more than wages. Enough to buy a little farm of your own, perhaps.' She was on her feet, going towards the kitchen. 'That's the kind of thing many want. Thing is, what we want costs money. This is our chance, and we can't take it without you. See what I mean?' I would be letting the side down. Comical. The last appeal anyone should make to me.

'There must be lots of chaps with experience of the North,' said Edward. 'Not just Mr Butler.' Yes. Officer chaps like yourself.

'Oh, I don't know. Not that many around here.' The bad angel in me. 'And once the chaps get settled in and Footner's humming again they won't want to leave, eh?' How I could use their own language to trick them. But even then I had no real intention of going anywhere with them. 'A profitable idea all round there. I think you should go, Edward.' Using his first name, as if we were old friends. He glanced up at me, and drew and drew on his cigarette. Did he think I was his friend? 'And to go with Mr Garrard here, an acknowledged expert on the North—how could it fail?'

'No.' So sharply and loudly I saw her husband flinch. 'Edward can't go. He can't, and you are not to advise him to go.' She was looking directly at me, her hand on the doorpost tightening. 'Harry can find other people.' I had got what I hadn't got otherwise this evening: her attention. It encouraged me to go on.

'A copper-bottomed idea. I shall have to think it over.'

That was an end of it. After a fashion. That was how it was, that evening: my provoking her only to get her attention again for one brief moment. But then I would say that, wouldn't I? I the liar, the thief, the adulterer, the murderer.

Edward led us to the recreation room, calling it that. Sarah brought in a tray with tea and brandy and glasses.

There it was again, that room with the bookcase and photographs of chums and relatives, the animal heads, the golf and cricket and tennis equipment, the fishing rods in racks. The piano with its photographs of young Sarah and her black spaniel, Edward the huntsman, squinting into the sun. How long ago? How many lives ago?

'Enough of the future for now.' Edward poured himself a brandy. 'Let us enjoy this evening.'

Harry Garrard picked a golf club out of the bag, puffed at the dust, swung the club, put it back. Swung the tennis racquet. 'Any chance of getting something going soon?' He was looking around at Edward, then at Sarah. 'No? Too early, I expect. Let it be a couple more months. I hear there used to be hunts here?' He was looking up at the mounted heads.

'Yes.' Edward. 'Not all shot by me, those,' he said. 'Well, none, actually. But cricket. I was more of a cricketer.' He was in one of the leather chairs, Sarah pouring tea for Harry. When she glanced at me, out of habit I expect, I did nothing but look back. She put down the pot and put the cosy on and moved away to the bookcase and straightened a photograph, fumbled at the books.

'I've been reading myself.' Harry, picking up on everything. 'There's a great thing I found in London last month. *Scott's Last Expedition.* Two volumes.' His upper so-white teeth moved out a little in his mouth and back in again. 'There were men. What risks they ran, appalling risks, and no

failure either, for they performed prodigies of human endurance, and the best men of all dead on the ice. Immortal renown, that's what they achieved—a first rate tragedy.'

And they continued to talk of Scott, or Harry Garrard
did. Because of course it was not an end of it, the change to
this talk of Scott, only more of the same.

How wise I was to know, the Irishman in the midst of these
English, that evening in the house in the hollow in the dry
burnt air of Footner, that all these 'best men' achieved was suffering and failure and death, that immortal renown was mean-
ingless, that nobody's business should lie with any kind of
tragedy. How superior I was, and yet it benefited me nothing.

I was riding towards Mrs Hudson's house and there was Sarah
walking on Centre Road with Hector, Harry Garrard and a tall
slim man. I swung the cayuse towards them. To be polite. To
be near Sarah. At the same moment Harry Garrard pointed
into the window of the closed-up butcher shop.

'Good morning, Mrs Underhill. Mr Garrard. Sir.' Only the
tall slim man turned. His suit hung on him, the hair beneath
the felt hat auburn and over-long. Sarah and Harry Garrard
still looking into the dusty, empty window. Sarah's behaviour I
expected. But Harry Garrard, who had hunted me out, was
avoiding me. 'All going well with your planning, I hope?'

'Ah. Mr Butler.' He swung around. 'Of course. Of
course.' Nodding, bare-headed still, the thick hair bouncing.
I looked down and waited. 'This is my old friend, Mr Charles
Critchell. Charles, Mr Butler. Another man who's lived, like
ourselves, in the North.'

'I've heard of you already, Mr Critchell.' I could remember little other than his name. 'You've travelled with Mr
Garrard, I hear?' Charles Critchell turned to Harry.

'Yes.' His hand went to a pocket. He took a handkerchief from it and held it clenched in his fist. 'Harry and I are old travelling friends.' There was an angry note in his voice. And all the time there was Sarah, aware, listening.

'I'm pleased to meet you.' I smiled at him. He mopped at the sweat on his forehead with the handkerchief. Sarah was walking away, along the street, to look into the window of the little clothes shop.

'Charles finds it too hot here, like myself.' Harry patted Charles on the back. 'We're all old ice men, aren't we, Charles? Never happier than when it's forty below.' Charles Critchell stared back at him. Whatever conversation I had interrupted hadn't been about how they enjoyed temperatures of forty below. 'Well, Charles and I have our own planning to do…'

'We certainly have,' said Mr Critchell.

Harry was leading his friend after Sarah. 'I hope you are still thinking about what came up the other night.' Called over his shoulder. And then I looked at Sarah again, along that hot dusty street, gazing in that petty clothes shop window at things she, no one, would ever buy.

At first I had been impatient, hungry, to hurry back after each day's work, in more of a hurry than ever, to sit on Mrs Hudson's porch and hope Sarah would come into town on her way to the Hotel, or riding Cap towards the Government Bridge. Or coming to look for me. She might, someday, come to look for me. I had not been in a hurry back for some time.

That evening I had put the cayuse away and washed up and was sitting down to Mrs Hudson's dinner when she said,

'Mrs Underhill has just been here, asking for you. I said you were often not home till after dark these evenings.' She talked on, of the evenings, of the weather, of something. But Sarah had called. Maybe memories had come to her of how it had been, how it had felt. Had seeing me ignited something—of course not what had been, but some sentiment I could work on, some way back in? My heart was singing, my foolish heart. What happened to hatred at that moment? And if we did meet again, be in love again, then even if it ended once more, if it really was not possible now Edward was home, I would be the one to leave. As if that would make a difference. I would go away and get that small farm in the west and find another woman, and I would be content. Such was in my foolish heart, in my foolish head.

At least now I could ride up to the house again, legitimately, and knock on the door. I wanted to go immediately, but Edward would be there, and Harry Garrard, and probably Charles Critchell. I ate hardly anything. I went to bed and lay there thinking of her, wondering, longing, killing hope as it came, reviving it again, over and over.

The next day I stayed about Mrs Hudson's or working in the Dunae yard. In the afternoon I saw both Harry Garrard and Charles Critchell on the Hotel porch, deep in talk. An hour later I saw Edward, riding Cap, heading for the Government Bridge. It was a gift, what I had been hoping for and not expecting. A sign, I almost thought. But there is no 'almost thought'. You think it or you don't. I might as well have said that god meant it to be. But I believed in no god then, and I know there is none now.

I galloped up to the porch, dropped the lines, ran, out of habit, to the back door. My singing, singing heart: this was what hope, unconfined, unconditional hope had felt like.

How wonderful, how frightening. I'd tell her I loved her. I'd say it, even if she didn't say it back. I would say it and she would know. I flung open the door. She was in the hallway, folded bedclothes in her arms. 'Sarah.' Then I saw the emotion on that strong face. It was not joy and pleasure and anticipation, and it was not love, but apprehension. She turned away, put the clothes down on the low table in the hall. When she turned back she had gathered herself.

'Thank you for coming to see me. So much… Would you mind… would you mind waiting on the porch? I'll bring out tea.'

It was not some glimpse of me, then, that had made her soften, a memory that had stirred longing, prompted her to try to work out something between Edward's presence and our—I still called it our—desire. She had some concern. I could guess what it was. Foolish and weak and needy I walked out and sat on the porch and waited, the dog and I, an inordinately long time for her to come with tea and cups and thin slices of cake that neither of us ate.

To sit across from her was a thing so familiar, so wonderful, and so upsetting. The words she was saying were ordinary, about tea, about being lucky to have this moment alone. Because it was her I valued them, these ordinary expressions I used to kiss her to stop her saying, until she too would become excited and want me as I wanted her.

'I am pleased you made it so soon,' she said. 'I wanted to talk to you about Edward.' So soon, to the point.

'Edward?' I could hear my disappointment, even though I thought I had prepared myself for just this disappointment.

'Yes. I wanted to be sure you wouldn't go to the North with him and Harry Garrard. He seems set on it, and it would be the end of him.' I said nothing. 'I wanted to be sure.'

She had lied for so long to Edward. Why couldn't she lie to me a little, give me some small hope? But I had to be given the truth, brutally, that she did not want Edward to go away again, and for us to have the long winter together, to be as before. For him to go to where he might never come back and be between us again. Maybe it was at that moment that I began to plan for that very thing.

'The gentleman you met on the street with us, Charles Critchell: it was Mr Critchell who put up the funding for himself and Harry to go into the Barrens before, on the promise of getting double his money back. They both nearly died. That is what he told me after our walk in town. Harry talks of it as if it were a game.'

'This has got nothing to do with me.' Yet I wanted her to keep talking. Even when it pained me.

'They lived in a hovel, a cave dug in a bank of icy rubble, Harry often not there but staying with other trappers, quarrelling with Indians until they beat him almost to death, no planning, badly equipped, freezing and starving for eight months.' She picked up her tea cup, the tea cup in those hands that had held me. Her fingertips, palms, inches away. I reached out and grasped her hand, and she looked away, along the open bench in front, towards the Thompson, as if someone might be walking or riding there but there might still be time for a kiss, but then she stood up and put her cup and saucer on the table and took herself away from me. 'And in the end any furs they got were of little worth because Harry hadn't cured and stored them properly.'

She paced about on the porch. I was moved by her, as I had been moved before by her concerns. I was angered too that they were for her husband and not for me.

'Edward's not well in different ways. It's not just his arm. He wants to get away from civilization as he calls it, as his cousin has encouraged him to call it, for a period of peace after his war. Maybe he's hoping for the comradeship of the trenches again. And to get away from me, I expect.' Her voice had fallen on her last words, and now she was silent, looking not at me but down at the floor. 'I shouldn't have told you those things. It's a betrayal of my husband. Of a good man.'

I liked her for that. I loved her anyway, but I liked her for that loyalty. I hated it too, for again it wasn't for me. I could feel the anger growing. Had she no thought for me, for what I might be thinking and feeling?

'Have you really been to the North?' she said.

'As your friend I'll do what I can.' As your friend—a phrase I would use too when it suited. I wouldn't let her see my anger. 'But I can't stop him going.'

'Harry says Critchell is just upset and exaggerating, that what furs they got were fine, that there never was an agreement to split the costs, and that the expedition didn't make money was due to the unusual circumstances of the season and nobody's to blame. Edward believes Harry. An old-Harrovian like his cousin wouldn't lie. He wants to have Critchell put out of the Hotel and back on a train. But you can see why Edward mustn't go anywhere with Harry.'

I stood up too.

'There's nothing I can do. I won't help them, if that's what you want.'

'Thank you.' But a quiet thank you that held no promise. 'Well, maybe there's no need to worry. Harry can't raise new funding anyway. He and his old chum are both leaving in the morning.'

I couldn't even pretend to be her friend any more, to get my mouth around those lying words. 'I must go.' I walked away across the porch. I wanted to look jaunty, easy, to whistle, but even I was neither that simple nor that much of a fraud.

In the days that followed I made plans, shared with no one, that I would draw my wages and savings and leave Footner. I would go west and find that place of my own. I would live my life. I would be wise. But there was another thought growing: if I went North with Edward I would be linked to Sarah through him. And that would trouble her, for she would never know what I might tell him. And this hatred, the passion to destroy, grew stronger as the other grew less, until one morning I woke up and knew, as though I had planned it overnight, that this day I was going to visit Edward and tell him that if Harry could raise the funding I would go with them, that I was his friend and would support him, that he could depend on me.

'You must do what you feel you should,' was his reply.

And in a week Harry was back. He had followed Charles Critchell to Calgary and somehow led him to believe that the way to get his lost money back was to invest the same again.

Let me tell you another thing. The thing that had come to me when the sun was like honey on the banks of the Thompson, when I saw Sarah's small pale feet, when Hector was almost swept away.

Wednesday, 18th October 1916, a date for which I need no notebook. Heavy rain had fallen all night but by dawn it had cleared and the sky was already warming up into sunlight. There wasn't a word being spoken in the barn. We were all sprawled on the straw or perched on buckets and churns, all of us smoking. I would hear the draw of breath and the paper smouldering down on a cigarette, and the exhalation, and then another draw of breath, so silent it was.

And silent and all, I never heard the door open. No sound, but the movement of somebody looking up. Then we all looked up. Standing in a cluster in the doorway were the six of them. Some of them turned, as if not to come in again after all, as if our world was not theirs any more. But like blood seeping under a door they would come in again. Those around me looked away then, at the stone flags of the floor, and the piles of equipment and straw and the flaring ends of cigarettes. I did not look away. The silence went on.

Suddenly a shout from the door. 'We did it.' One foolish broken shout into the silence, the door banged back against the wall. Then they all came in, boots grating, grinding, on the stone floor, the door left open behind them, the low sunlight streaming past them and the straw motes dancing. Johnny Laister, the one who had shouted, threw himself on the straw, face down, cap still on.

'Cigarettes,' said Arthur Baines. 'Give me a fucking cigarette.' He looked around, and crossed to my blanket and without asking picked up my packet of Woodbines and took one and passed the packet to the others. They lit the Woodbines, standing in the middle of the barn. They drew on them, blew the smoke into the air, and behind the smoke the motes faded, and the smoke fell, and the motes danced again.

'I had the blank one.' Charlie Wright. They were moving apart already. 'I could tell by the bloody weight.'

'Lying bastard.' Arthur Baines. The long draw on the cigarette. Still holding my packet of Woodbines. The long exhalation. 'I had it.'

'Some one of us had it. As long as one of us had it.' Charlie Wright.

'It might have been somebody from the other platoon.' Brian Rooney. His voice hardly audible.

Thirty seconds of silence. The rustle of straw.

'There is no blank one.' Johnny Laister. Still face down, hiding his tears.

Others with nothing to say. Nothing to be said.

Charlie Wright walked away to the dirty window and stood looking out at the brightening sky. Under it, a mile away, the place in the trees where in a dawn breaking after rain an officer had pinned an envelope to the chest of a poor terrified wretch of a man. Where these men had done what they had been ordered to do, where afterwards the officer had done what he had been ordered to do, stepping forward with his Webley as if twelve rifle shots might not be enough.

'We'll be somewhere else soon.' Brian Rooney. 'It'll be in the past soon.'

'Ha ha. We'll all be dead soon.' Arthur Baines.

'We got a day's leave,' said Charlie Wright. There was a roaring sound and the splash of his vomit hitting the stones.

None of the rest of us, we who had not been drawn, had, it seemed to me, taken a breath since they had come back to the barn.

'Michael Furey,' said the voice from the straw. 'What are *you* looking at? You would have done the same. Wouldn't you?' He was staring hard and angry into my eyes. 'Wouldn't you?'

'Yes,' I said. Then loudly, to show I wasn't afraid, 'Yes,' and it was at that moment I knew I was going to leave them and my own country and my own name and find a place far away where I would take orders from no man ever again. Not because I was different, but because I was not different.

Because I was ordinary. Because I was as they were: ignorant, scared, and so biddable.

Later what I remembered most often, because it was all I wanted to remember, were the motes dancing in the sunlight, and disappearing behind the cigarette smoke, and reappearing and disappearing all over again.

CHAPTER TWELVE

IT CAME ABOUT AS HARRY SAID, FOR A WHILE. We took that train to Edmonton, stayed in the Adamson Corona Hotel, where old trappers and miners who knew Harry kept turning up, all lauding him. He handed out copies of a photograph of himself sprawled in the snow with a cup of tea. Then one old trapper took me aside and told me of Harry having to be fed by Indians to pull through the winter. A young woman, surprisingly attractive, came, and took several long walks with Harry. Charlie Chaplin and Edna Purviance. Eventually he bought a Chestnut canoe, a McClary stove, two rifles (but no shotgun), red Hudson's Bay blankets, traps, food (but not enough), other things we needed, like a capote (but not three of them). We took that Muskeg Express to Waterways, Harry complaining it was too late to see the 'real North', that now it was full of towns and boats and families and government surveyors. Waterways had a dozen houses and two women, both native. We 'threw' the canoe in the Athabasca, and from that moment on there was no way to turn back, and nothing to be done but stick it out through the winter, and hope for the best. That, in the depths of my bad heart, I wished to be the death of Edward and the devastation of Sarah. As if that would make me important to her again.

By October we were in a ramshackle twelve foot by twelve foot cabin built by Harry two years before on a bend of the Thelon River, the roof bowed with soil and gravel. There was a stand of black spruce behind us, until we cut almost all of them down for firewood, and a flat white frozen world around us. We had to go beyond where anyone else would go, he said, for there the greater rewards would lie. The temperature dropped to17°F, fifteen degrees of frost, rose to 26°F a few days later, to plunge again to 14°F. A strong north wind blew and kept blowing. By the end of November it was − 10°F, forty-two degrees of frost, and falling, and we were already almost out of food. We had killed four caribou on the way up river, but there hadn't been one near the cabin where Harry had told us they would be passing in droves, for us to shoot forty at least and store for the winter. Not one of the musk ox he had talked of. We had trapped about thirty white fox, not the hundreds he had promised. We had a pet fox, until we killed and ate it. We struggled through to Christmas and the New Year, weakening, gulping down a ptarmigan or wolverine for one meal and starving on flour and sugar for the next week. On and on. I had hit my foot with the axe, and it wasn't healing. I had shot no animals, only taking dead ones from the traps, but I would have gladly shot or strangled or cut the throat of anything that walked or flew by then. I hated and feared every minute of every day.

And every day I looked at Edward and thought: at a time and place of my choosing I will tell you of Sarah and myself, and every day from then on, every night, you will look at me and know that I, your wife's lover, knew her as you never did. And another who knows her as you never did may well be with her now, while you and I, a pair of fools, are here. Would it torture him any more than it tortured me? And every day I put it off and saved it for another, weaker, more needy-again day.

When I did tell him I regretted it. I have never ceased to regret it. Now Harry Garrard was dead, and Edward was dying, and the temperature had been −17°F the last time I had bothered to look.

Sometime in the afternoon I heard Edward move in his bunk. There was still some heat in the stove, and I made tea.

I brought this to him with our last three aspirin. He was sitting up, quiet and very drained. He made no move to take the tea. It was as if he hadn't seen me, and then he reached out and took the cup.

'Thank you,' he said. He drank the tea, the aspirin lying on his blankets.

'Take them.' I pointed to the aspirin. He didn't. I didn't know what I should do, so I began to talk. 'Soon, in a month or two, we'll be back in Footner.' I was thinking of Sarah of course, but that brought more pain than solace, and it might be the same for Edward. 'It'll be warm there. It's warm there now. The trees will be in blossom—' He raised his hand. He sat looking towards the foot of his bunk, and I thought he had forgotten about me.

Then, 'This is kind of you, Jack. You are good to me.' We sat on in silence. 'Have you...?' he began. He sat up farther and looked over at Harry's bunk, and answered the question for himself. 'No. We still have to lay him out. We have to do things right.'

'I didn't want to disturb your sleep.' I didn't want to touch Harry's corpse until I had to. 'Take the aspirin. Rest some more before we do anything.'

'We have to do things right,' said Edward again. His face was white beneath the grime and beard. His hands were shaking. I couldn't see him doing much of anything again. I got to my feet.

'You lie down, Edward. I'll do whatever's to be done for Harry.' I would, to get it over with. And maybe because Edward was owed whatever little peace there was. 'But lie and rest, if you can't sleep.' He put the three aspirin in his mouth one after another, and chewed them slowly, and I stood with him until he was finished. 'Lie down. Soon I'll cut wood, and there is some of the fish and bone left for you. But I'll attend to Harry first.' He lowered himself into the blankets. 'Why don't you turn your face to the wall?' He did, but I went back and sat on the box again.

I was thinking of Sarah. Of how she had lied and misled me. And of how she had given me her wonderful body. Her companionship. Our talks together. Her on horseback on the bench lands on a still late autumn evening, talking of when we had first met. Talking of a lie. One of mine.

'When you said, that morning in Kamloops, that you were going to the west to enlist, I knew you were lying. You were never going to enlist. You were not going to war.' I had stayed silent, curious, and feeling no surprise either that she had seen this in me. 'This unshaven Irish chap with the cut on the side of his head, who had slept in the bushes the night before. The wisest man I had met in three years. Of course that drew me to you. That was why I asked you to Footner and offered you a place to stay.' She moved on ahead, and then said back over her shoulder, 'That, and that you could help us work the orchards until the men returned. Those who would return.' She had paused there, perhaps waiting for me to say something, but what could I have said? 'Edward must have his farm. I owe him that.'

I thought of it now, her telling me, and my passing it over and not reacting, because I wasn't really taking it in. Because I was in love with her. Because I wanted her to be in love with me.

But what had that been if not a warning? How, really, had she lied and misled me?

It was dark before I rose. I lit one of the fox fat candles, and by its guttering yellow light stooped to where Edward had stored clothes in a parcel underneath his bunk. I picked out of it a dirty but good quality shirt, one of the expensive Copeland's he had brought back from England, and worn in the long-ago summer. The initials A.N.U., his father's I supposed, were monogrammed on the pocket. I took it to Harry's bunk. I looked at that toothless mouth and withered lips and those reddened eyes. After this I wouldn't have to look at them again. I raised the head and the bony shoulders and wrapped the shirt around his head, and tied the sleeves beneath his chin. I was exhausted by this, but now I had started I wanted to continue while Edward slept, so I rested for ten or fifteen minutes and went on.

I pulled the Hudson's Bay blankets back from him, bones and filth falling away. Then I took one of the greasy blankets and spread it on the floor beneath the bunk. I made myself grasp him by the shoulders and trailed him off the bunk onto the blanket. Beneath the thick trousers, the wrappings of bits of blanket he had tied around himself, the wool shirts and the tweed jacket, he was nothing but bone. I was glad, for otherwise I would not have been able to move him at all. I wrapped the blanket around him and tied it with packing twine.

When I had rested again I took the bottom end and tugged him over the earth floor towards the door. I tumbled him outside into the darkness, and trailed him the last few feet towards the side away from the small window. I got him close and parallel to the wall, and left him. The snows would cover him and freeze him solid. I crept inside again, to the little pool of flickering yellow candlelight.

I took the candle to my bunk, and lay down, my head spinning, my heart pounding. As I lay on my side I looked at that little candle flame, flickering up, shuddering in drafts, becoming straight again. I had been frightened and unhappy so often here, but never more so than at that moment, and part of it was fear and sorrow for Edward. Then I put my lips closer to the flame, and felt the warmth around my mouth, and puffed, and it went out, and I slept.

When I awoke it was daylight and Edward was up and moving about the cabin. He was barely able to stand.

'Thank you for all you have done,' he said. 'I wasn't up to it.' He crossed the floor towards the table to where his notebook lay, and slumped down onto the tin trunk, his heavy clothing hanging around him. 'I have looked outside,' he said.

'Are you satisfied?' I was still in my bunk, not wanting to rise and face whatever the day held.

'Did you read anything?' he asked. I thought he meant the notebook, and said quickly,

'No. No, of course not.'

He thought for a while. 'Or just say something, maybe?'

'No.'

There was silence again.

'I have a Bible.'

'Why don't you put on the capote?'

'Then I wouldn't feel the good of it when I went out.' His mouth opened and he made a small and brief laughing sound. His face flushed. 'You know, I never said it to Harry, not wanting to hurt his feelings, but there was something a little old-fashioned about his idea of bravery; no enemies but cold and starvation, sacrifice that involved no death but one's own.' He looked away, into the cabin wall, and beyond it, with a flicker of the little smile he had on first coming home. 'That's not how it can be, now.' He was very still. 'A whole war stands between us and all that.'

I got out of bed.

'Why don't you let me get you something to eat? There is still a wolverine hide.'

'I don't feel hungry,' he said. 'Later.' I rested on the box at the end of the table, and after a while went on and lit the stove, and while the water boiled I cut strips of hide and pounded them for softening as best I could. It seemed an insurmountable amount of work.

'What Harry said... another in the room, watching us?' He spoke slowly. 'For me, too. But it is not death.' I kept pounding on the hide and said nothing. 'Another.' Of course he could mean only Sarah. I looked over at him. He was lying on his side, watching me, the flicker of the little smile still there.

That day we ate what we could of the wolverine hide. We could never manage much. We both had constipation and cramps, our stomachs and intestines distended with gas. Harry had been right, we said. I watched Edward, his eyes often closed, pain crossing his face, sweat running down his cold forehead. Little moans would escape him, and he would apologise. 'Sorry, old boy,' and before he had finished his silly English exclamation his face would contort again.

At times he spoke in short bursts.

'It's a theatre. That's what this is. This scene. We, the cast. The wind, the snow, the effects. Our costumes. Our speeches.

'The wild things of no man's land. Savages. The ghouls who live underground. That's what we are.

'Things come in threes... haven't you thought that? Numbering off... one, two, three. Front, Support, Reserve. Sleep, food, a woman, in that order. And us wounded... man, animal, then corpse.

'I had a talisman. A little ribbon Sarah had in her hair the day I left. Carried it all through the War. Lost it in Edmonton on the way up. Isn't that odd? Isn't that odd?'

'Edward. You need an enema.' His face remained twisted but his head shook.

'No.' Through his clenched teeth. The gold tooth glinting far back in that dark mouth. 'I know how you feel about that.'

I got out of my bunk. I got the funnel and rubber tube and the bowl, and warmed water, and melted fox grease.

'Yes, Edward.'

And I did. Pulling down his filthy tweed trousers, the undergarments none of us had fully removed since November, inserting the tube. If I had not wanted to do it for him I wouldn't have. I saw his eyes fill with tears, the pain again I supposed, then he grasped my hand, and said, 'Thank you. Thank you.' I don't know if it helped. I want to think it did.

In the next days I searched more and more in the dumps. Edward became weaker and weaker, lying on his bunk, moaning with cramps, always trembling. All around us the cold went on and on, with no sign of any break, with no animals coming north, with nothing better in sight.

I came back from digging with the axe, and found Edward lying on the frozen earth floor of the cabin, not able to get up. In his hand was the pencil, on the table the open notebook. I put down my bowl of offal and got him to his feet and sat him on the edge of his bunk.

'It's good you can still get about,' he said. I put blankets over his shoulders.

'Yes.' What if we both were as he was, with nothing to be done except watch each other weaken further and die? 'I'm a few years younger. I suppose that makes a difference.'

'Of course. You are younger,' said Edward. 'But you have your injured foot.'

'It's no better, but no worse.' My injured foot had saved me from all the long, exhausting and useless excursions that Harry had led Edward on. That, I believed, was why I was in better health. 'I am not in great shape, Edward.' Then, knowing it would have sounded to him like self-pity, 'But I am grateful for the health I have.'

'Your injury was not your fault, Jack.'

Of course it was my fault. Not an act of God, to teach me a lesson.

'I'll light the stove. When I go out I should leave enough wood for you to keep it going longer. Then I'll cook up these things.'

That was my experience of the North. I had been a cook in a mining camp at Whitehorse.

All Edward could manage was a cupful of the greasy water. When he didn't take the bits of intestine I put in front of him I chopped them up smaller and smaller, and pushed them into his mouth and made him swallow. All the time his notebook lay open on the table where he had left it. While he lay with his face to the wall I read his last page. For once it was not notes on the weather or the failure of hunting. The writing was more childish but still regular and legible. He had written:

Sarah. My Sarah. I should never have taken you to Footner. Never left you there. I should have been more brave and not gone to war. I could not talk of that, of when I wasn't with you. But I could have told you I loved you, had always loved you, would always love you. You are all the world to me. My whole existence. I should have told you that.

It would be the last thing he would write.

When he couldn't eat now I'd put his food into my mouth, chew it, then take it out and push it into his. Once I swallowed his food, purposely, in front of him, and licked my lips and showed him my empty mouth. I looked back into his uncomplaining eyes.

Very soon after another change took place in him.

On the morning of April 27th I rose, feeling better than I had a week previously. That was a rare, rare feeling. I was setting the fire when I heard a groan from Edward. He seemed to be struggling to sit up. He tried to vomit, but there was nothing to vomit. He fell back onto the bunk again. I came and stood beside him.

'Would you like water? The stove will soon be going, and there will be some.'

He shook his head.

'My left side,' he said. 'I can't...' His voice fell away. 'There was something in my head.'

'A pain?'

'No. Like a sound.' His eyes were closed. 'It woke me up. Not a sound. A feeling.' He seemed to go to sleep again, and I left him, and got the best bits I could find on the table, some fish guts and weasel bones, and boiled them and pounded them up to make a little stew. I sat with him, trying to wake him to eat, but when he opened his eyes he shook his head, and fell back into sleep again.

Another day went by with Edward not leaving his bunk at all, drinking a little greasy water now and then, but hardly talking except sometimes about the uselessness of his left side. It was then I realized he had most likely had a stroke on April 27th.

On the morning of May 2nd when I woke he was already awake.

'Jack,' he said. I went across to him. 'I think I have shaken off that chill.' He was nodding, his eyes flicking about quickly, more alert than anytime in the past week. 'I still don't seem to be very strong, but I feel better. I know I'm better.' All the features of his face were so sharp and angled, the skin a dreadful colour in the morning light. He was twisting in his bunk as if trying to get up. 'No,' he said. 'I can't get up now. But later, maybe.'

'Of course,' I lied to him. 'Sure you will.' If it helped him I would speak of her after all. 'Soon, a month, two months at most, you'll be back with Sarah in Footner.' What did it matter? 'Those things I said… about Sarah.' I wanted to salve my own conscience, I suppose. It was selfishness, not goodness. 'They weren't true. Believe that. I was jealous. I was looking for someone to hurt…'

'No.' His hand moved a little, barely rising, but his voice was strong and determined. 'The evening I came home to Footner… we talked. I played the piano, badly. I fell asleep. She helped me to bed. When I awoke she had slept in the bunkhouse.' He rested, took several deep breaths. 'Of course I moved there. Of course she must do what she needs to do. When you told me of you and her I—'

'I lied—' I started to say again, uselessly.

'I was hurt. But it wasn't unexpected. Footner is a small town. That was one reason why I didn't want you to come to the North. It was obvious poor Harry wasn't all that was claimed for him.'

In this ugly place I knew he was telling the truth, as he had known when I had spoken of Sarah and myself. I sat in silence. Then, as uselessly, 'Can I get you anything?'

'So there was no reason for someone Sarah cared about, who cared about her, to risk death too.'

'Edward…' There was nothing I could add.

'Water,' he said. 'I could drink water.'

'I'll get the stove going.'

I was carrying bits of board to the stove when he spoke again. 'There's one more thing. That poem of Byron's. I looked it up. Don Juan.' I fed wood into the stove, waited for him. 'And read on. There were other lines, which she hadn't quoted to me either. Like this… Listen. "In her first passion a woman loves her lover."' How he watched me so intently. '"In all the others… all she loves is love."' There was a grin on the hollow face. I straightened. 'What do you think of that?' And he gave a little laugh. 'Where does that leave us chaps, eh?'

One criticism of Harry, one flash of unmediated bitterness for me. I felt all the more for him: another vulnerable, beaten, human animal. Later I brought him the water, and held it for him to drink, but he took hardly any. I left, as I had to, trailing the axe behind me, to dig and search.

I had fox bones with me when I came back. I lit the stove and worked on the fox, and when I had boiled the bones for a while I put some in a bowl and went back to sit by Edward's bunk. I looked down at him, watching the slight rise and fall of his chest, the small movements around his mouth.

I dropped a fox bone on the floor, and bent to pick it up. As I straightened and looked back at Edward I realised he was no longer breathing. I put the bowl down, got to my feet. I leant over and looked at his face, now so still. Was he really dead? I put my cheek down to his mouth but there was nothing to feel.

I sat there looking at him, suddenly sadder than I had ever expected to feel, or to have strength to feel. I reached over and touched his eyelids and closed them. There was no more I could do. I had little strength and no will for more. I blew out the candle and sat in the darkness, with only the faint dying glow from the stove. The cold was descending, hunger as always with me, and I had not Harry's will, nor Edward's. I wanted to lie down. At that I remembered Harry's words:

'All I want to do is sleep, and if I sleep I'll not want to awaken.'

But mad Harry was wrong, for after a long and deep and dreamless sleep light was in the cabin, and I was awake, and Edward was dead in the bunk opposite, and Harry frozen stiff in a red blanket outside. I made myself rise. There was the gnawed and chopped at wolverine hide, and sucked fox bones, and no firewood. I went to Edward's bunk and pulled the end of his tartan blanket over his face. I tried to pick him up by the shoulders, to trail him off the bunk onto the earth floor, as I had with Harry, but I hadn't the strength. I stopped, rested, and then rolled him off onto the floor. He hit the hard earth with barely a sound, still tangled in the blanket, partly on his face. I tucked the blanket in around him and tied it here and there with bits of packing twine as I had done with Harry.

I trailed the body to the door, in fits and starts, bumped him over the step and into the snow, and tugged him along until I could leave him beside Harry. I stood there, slumped over, exhausted, finished. They had ended up head to toe. I went back in again. I lit a fire, pulled the supports out of Edward's bunk, stuck them into the stove and sat there, drained of all will, all ability. I would again, I knew, go to the dumps and scratch at the snow and earth with the axe head. I would take the rifle outside, on the off chance that some animal would come close enough, and stay long enough, for my wobbling hands to raise the rifle in its general direction and get off a shot. But right now all I could do was sit and stare into the flames of the stove.

CHAPTER THIRTEEN

ALL THE TIME I WAS THINKING OF THE BODIES outside in the snow. That day I left them alone, but I knew I would not leave them alone for ever. Yet neither could I bring myself to go as far as the dumps that day. I ate what I could of the wolverine hide and lay down again. I was beaten, the spirit gone.

The next morning I got up, as slowly as ever. I went outside, and raised my head. The sky was the same relentless unbroken grey. I crept past the two stiff and partly snow-covered bundles beside the cabin, and went to the dumps as so often before. That day I was lucky: I chopped out of the refuse a fat wolverine gut and kidneys and heart, and as I was about to come away I found a fox gut. This was more food than I'd had in days. The idea of that buoyed me up. As I came back to the cabin I hardly saw the two bundles. The guts and kidneys and heart would support me. I would keep finding offal with sufficient food value to set me on my feet. I would get about enough to accumulate firewood. I would watch for birds passing overhead. The spring would come. Animals would return. I would eventually be able to take out the rifle and hope for a kill. I would eat. The two bundles would remain as they were.

No animals came. No birds flew north. The winter had not gone.

But as I dug deeper in the refuse dumps I found better value offal and bones. How hard the early days of winter had seemed. How plentiful they seemed now I was living on what we had thrown away then. And it was only I living on it.

I had both rifles loaded and set beside the door, so that if I heard something I would be in a position to shoot at it. While I felt I was getting more than before from the refuse my joints were jerking in and out of position as I moved. There was the sensation of bone grinding on bone. My wrists were like larch twigs, my thighs like bed poles. I had no muscle bulk, certainly no body fat for warmth.

Before Harry died I had thought that we were taking twice or three times as long to do everything. By now I would have estimated it as five or six times as long. If I did not set out early to cross the hundred yards or so to the dump, scrape around, drop whatever it was into the bowl, it would be dark before I made it back to the cabin. Getting the stove going in the mornings took over two hours, even if I had firewood laid in from the day before. Sometimes I would get it going, to find that by the time I trailed wood across the cabin it was out again. Sometimes I would waken and find it still dark, and I wouldn't know if I had slept through the daylight, or if it was the same night I had gone to bed, and so I lost track of the days.

I burned the rest of the cache. I burned the fox furs. I flicked through Edward's few books, the Robert Service poetry and the Bible I had never seen him read, his *Birds of Canada*. I burned them all. I put his notebook in the stove, then pulled it out again. I opened Harry's suitcase and burned his clothes. In the bottom was an evening suit, black tie, dress shirt and a set of gold studs. I burned those clothes too, and then the suitcase. I found and burned his white teeth.

And I thought of what I had done, enabling Edward to come North to die. And another man too, not evil, only weak and foolish and vain. And I thought of Sarah, her whom I had loved, not as I should but selfishly, jealously, possessively. As something other than human, when none of us, even her, were anything more than poor creatures of clay, stumbling around in this morass. I had lost hatred, and with it that self-ish, destructive desire I had called love.

Or maybe I was lying. Maybe I longed for her as much as ever, and underneath my rationalizations I knew it.

Around May 10th I looked out of the small window as darkness came down, and four ptarmigan were searching for food in the dying light between the cabin and the river. I got the rifle and opened the door. The birds didn't move. I stepped out of the doorway to come closer. They had seen me now and were alert and taking off and landing again. I fired one shot, the recoil of the rifle knocking me over. When I looked up from the snow all the birds had flown. I had got nothing, but these were the first animals of any kind I had seen for a long time. More would come. At that moment I thought again of Harry's refusal to buy a shotgun, and the rage I had felt about him swept over me as fresh as ever. The bastard. The fool. The murderer of his own cousin, and the murderer of me, if I let it happen.

I saw what I had just thought as if the words were written in the snow. If I let it happen... but if I only had enough pluck I would pull through. How comical it was. If I'd had the strength I would have laughed. Then I laughed anyway. No sound came but I lay in the snow and laughed until my dry eyes ached. I got up and went back inside.

Every day now I was crawling from cabin to dump, to lie digging in the snow, my head spinning, vision blurred, feet and hands frozen. Then crawling back, my clothes soaking. It brought on a heavy chill. I would lie in my bunk sweating, and then suddenly becoming cold again, so much so that all the coverings I could find would not warm me. This, I remembered well, was what had happened to Harry before he died. But I would still make myself get out and crawl across the snow, and dig and scrape and scavenge. *Non recuso laborem.* The idea of eating from the two bundles at the door hardly ever left my mind, and at the same time I kept telling myself that was what I would do when I was *in extremis.* And, I convinced my starved, exhausted, ill and dying self, I was not *in extremis* yet.

Sometimes the weather was warmer, a comparatively mild 25°F, or seven degrees of frost. The digging at the dumps grew easier as the ground softened. The other side of that was that the scraps and offal went off in the spells when the temperatures rose enough to briefly thaw them out. My body was no guide to the real temperature, but eventually I realized that my chill had largely left me, and that I was still alive.

I calculated, as best I could, that it was around May 14th. The next day, then, Harry's lauded first day of spring. As I looked out the tiny cabin window that night I could see snow falling heavily. I went to bed and took one of the longest sleeps of my life. When I awoke it was late in the following afternoon. I had slept through most of the supposed first day of spring. I burned the last of the table, ate again at the terrible wolverine hide, and slept into May 16th.

That day I got out, trailing myself about in the soft fresh snow. I returned to the cabin while it was still light. I had some scraps in the bowl but I wanted, needed, something more. I took the knife and went outside again and knelt in the snow beside the blanket where Edward was wrapped. After a while I lay down in the snow, too weak, or unwilling, for the moment to undo the covering. My eyes closed. I was aware I would die if I stayed here. How much would I care? Mad Harry was right. The will to live would go.

I slept. When I opened my eyes I was on my back, looking upward into the late afternoon sky, at the dark grey of the clouds, at the paler clouds showing here and there behind the dark. And as I watched the clouds parted a little. There was the merest patch of blue sky visible. I lay and watched it. The blue spread.

And then I saw the most wondrous thing I have ever seen. In the clear blue air a swan was making its way across the sky. Going north. Hundreds of feet up, a pure white swan in the pure blue sky. A swan, its long neck outstretched, its great wings beating. From Edward's book I knew this was a whistling swan, on its way to its breeding grounds. It was spring. At that I rose again and crept back into the cabin. I would make another day. I told myself that Harry and Edward were nothing but more bone anyway.

The next day I woke, and was working on my knees at the stove, trying to coax it to life, to cook the bone and skin I had rejected the night before, when I heard thumping sounds outside. They calmed, then came again. I crept to the door, reached up, tugged the wooden latch, and let the door swing open. I looked out into the bright air. Four or five caribou had come down the side of the hill behind the cabin, and were starting to cross the frozen river. As I watched one put his hoof through the ice. Whether it was the condition of the ice that distracted them or not I did not know, but they didn't seem to be aware of me. I picked up the .303, and toppled sideways with the weight of it. I righted myself, lying in the doorway, panting, my heart fluttering. When I looked up the caribou had almost crossed the river and were scrabbling out of the ice on the other side. I tried to point the rifle but I could not raise it properly. I crawled on outside, and raised myself on my elbows. The caribou were gone. I began to sob. My life had been put in front of me, and then taken away again. I lay there, my head in the snow, the rifle forgotten.

Then I heard the thumps again, more than before, closer, and the snorts and puffs of animals. I raised my head slowly. Twenty, thirty, forty maybe, caribou were in the process of crossing the river about forty yards away. They were as oblivious to me as I had been to them until now. I raised the rifle and fired from where I lay. I just fired into them, and thought myself lucky to get off the shot. Immediately the recoil battered into my thin shoulder. But somehow I pulled the bolt back and put another round into the chamber. The herd were scrabbling at the breaking ice. I fired again, in that same unfocused way. The butt hit my shoulder again and I passed out.

When I came to the herd was long since gone. But two caribou lay dead, one on the snow, one partly on the ice. Two caribou. I lay for another hour before I could crawl to the nearest with the knife.

I thrust the knife at its stomach. Tears came to my eyes. I couldn't penetrate the skin. I tried again. Nothing. I leant on the knife handle with all my weight, and felt the knife go in. Then I hacked with it, until the stomach opened. The contents spilled out, chewed moss, semi-digested. I picked up handfuls and ate it. I cut again at the stomach, going lower and further into the body now I was past the tough skin. I was hunting for the liver, and I found it, and took it out and ate it raw and still warm.

I could feel my life return to me. I lay there, blood on my hands, blood on my face, blood and food in my body. I dozed, awoke, vomited up what I had eaten, and ate again.

I lied to you. A sin not of omission but commission. All that time ago, a lifetime, coming up onto the first streets of Kamloops on that April morning, I did stop and look back. Even then, after a glimpse, I was aching to see her again. Down over the rail yard and the lines, and the long train clanging, and there she was, going away on the path by the river. I thought about her, wondered about her, longed for her, this woman. Where did she live, how did she live, what did she do when she was not walking in a white shimmering dress by the river and the rail lines so early in the morning?

I watched her walk away, the long train slowly passing her, and the tired clink and clack of the wagons and the slow clang of the bell passing her. I watched her until she entered the shadows beneath the red bridge and I could see her no more, and I felt the vacancy in my heart.

On Saturday, 11th September 1920 I got off a train in Footner, a weak stick of a man with a bad foot, the clothes I had strode off in hanging on me. There was a CPR man, a stranger, on the station platform, looking at me as if I was an oddity, and no one else around. In my hand was the suitcase I had stored in the Adamson Corona Hotel in Edmonton, my few toilet things and Edward's notebook rattling in it.

From the canoe on the thawing Thelon River to Baker Lake, to Churchill, in the boarding houses, on the trains to Saskatoon, to Edmonton, to here, I saw myself stepping down onto the platform, walking directly out to the house in the hollow and up to her door and knocking. I too had been to the mountain top, conquered something in myself, become what I was not before. She would have learned of Edward's death long since from newspapers. She would have learned of my survival. She would open the door, cry for Edward, and I would do my duty. I would give her his notebook, and she would know then what she had meant to him. I would tell her what a man he was, more brave and clear-sighted than I had ever acknowledged, a hero. Some day I would be old, as even Sarah would be old, but for Edward there would be no more ageing. Then duty done, I would be free. Free of jealousy. Free of hatred. Free of un-reciprocated love. Of Sarah, the name I had given to my emptiness and longing.

I was still lying.

There was nobody on the street. I started to cross the road, and there was the Hotel, the porch dusty and empty of chairs, the doors closed and curtains drawn on all the upper windows. I was turning away when I saw Miss Weir at one of the ground floor windows watching me. I stepped up onto the porch and stopped opposite her.

'Good day, Miss Weir.' I meant it. Good day, to a woman who had lost her brother, who for whatever reason—money, pride, determination to honour him—had trapped herself in a failing business in a failing town. I expected no reaction but a snub, but she pointed to her left, to the corner of the Hotel. I heard a door open at the side, and there she stood, straight-backed, greying hair tightly in a bun. The black ribbon still on her arm. I followed her into her sitting room. Carpeted, heavy mahogany furniture. The portrait photograph of Gordon over the fireplace, draped in the black crepe ribbon. A sabre on the wall, beside it an upright lance with its pennant spread. There was a scrapbook open on a small side table.

She made tea, and while she was gone I turned the pages of the scrapbook, reading the cuttings from the *Ashcroft Journal* and the *Inland Sentinel*, the *Globe*, the *Times* of London. Gordon winning the Victoria Cross races. The 31st British Columbia Horse, August 27th 1914, boarding a train at Kamloops, a massive crowd in attendance, the last time she would have seen him. The incident of Gordon's death in a cavalry charge against machine guns. The commendation of his superior officer. Gordon's award of the Victoria Cross.

She came back with her cups and saucers. She asked me nothing about Harry Garrard or Edward Underhill or about myself. She gave me sentences of news:

'Eric my brother and my sister Audrey came on a visit. Very enjoyable to see them again.

'I'm afraid all your work on the flume has been undone. A storm in April left it in very bad shape. Practically collapsed in places. Hardly any Chinese boys around now, of course.

'But then you won't have your job, unfortunately. BCHEC has sold out to a man in Vancouver. We haven't had the privilege of a visit yet.

'We have lost two of our oldest residents. Our dear Major Sidgwick has gone to live with his son in Victoria. Old Mr Woolley has passed away. He has a very nice grave in Ashcroft.

'Mrs Hudson and Jameson the telegram and newspaper boy... some were not surprised.

'Miss Fanny Ricketts has left to marry a man in Ontario.'

All I wanted to hear about was Sarah.

'And Mrs Underhill?' She was looking down into her cup. She swirled the pale tea. 'And how is Mrs Underhill?' She looked up, and there was the little smile of old there, and I understood why I had been invited into her parlour, why I had been offered tea, told all else of Footner except this thing she must know I desired most of all. 'Tell me.'

'No need to raise your voice, Mr Butler.' She drank tea, lowered her cup slowly. 'Mrs Underhill is dead.' A confirming nod of the head. 'She drowned in the Thompson. Her poor dog too, both swept away. In the last week of April, just after the storms. Her boater hat was found at the little beach,

Juniper Beach some call it, but their bodies were never found. No. Neither of them.' I was on my feet. 'They say the dog might have been swimming, and was carried off, and perhaps she went in to try to save it. No one knows, really. She was there on her own. She'd just had all that lovely hair cut off, too. Some, not myself of course, say she may have… after all…'

I was gone, out of the door. I ran, walked and ran again, limping along Centre Road. A cry came from a porch: 'Jack—' I spun round, as if it could be her, knowing it wasn't her. Terry Sullivan, the CPR man, stepping down from the porch of Mrs Hudson's house, his newspaper and mug of tea beside the chair where I had sat and longed for a glimpse of my Sarah. 'Jack… hold on…' I kept running. She was dead. I came over the hill at last, legs hardly able to carry me, and down into the yard. I ran because I wanted to think this was some cruel joke from Miss Weir, her whose brother was dead, who would want everybody to think they had lost those dearest to them, and I would find it out. This cruel joke. But there was no horse in the corral, no borrowed Gray-Dort at the door. No one on this porch.

I stood there, panting, longing, aching. My Sarah. I stepped up onto the porch. The pots of geraniums were still there, dead brown sticks. I took the key and opened the door. There was dust in the hall, a cobweb on the hunting prints. I went past the bedroom, the big mahogany bed with its covers tidily made up, waiting for a sleeper, waiting for those making love. The kitchen, with an unopened can of salmon on the table. No CPR men, no Canadians from Savona or Ashcroft, had taken the house, the land, here. The parlour, the big leather chairs. The silver things along the book cases. On the rug in front of the fireplace a gasoline can.

I picked it up and shook it. About half full. A box of Swan Vestas fell from the top. I picked up the box, opened it, as if there would be something inside, a note from her, some secret information of where she had gone. Only red-topped matches. I lowered myself into the chair beside the fireplace. Her chair. Where her body had sat, while she waited for me.

Someone had come in here, after she was missed. Who knew of the key under the flowerpot.

Had she told the story of the gasoline can and the remittance men in the Okanagan to someone else? Then it struck me. Her new lover. The man I had persuaded myself did not exist. But here was the can, the matches. He, whoever he was, had come in here after her death. He had sat in this chair and thought the thoughts I was thinking now… her chair, where her body had sat while she waited for him.

But…

In the early summer… before she could have known anything of the fates of Edward and Harry and myself… she had come to the beach and waded in. That's what they said. She had come to Juniper Beach with Hector and left her hat, and waded in. Where we had seen the drowned cow. Where she had sworn she would never enter the water again. Where she would most certainly never let Hector enter the water again. In April, in the fast flow after the storm.

She would know I would know that.

There was no other lover.

I sat there and sat there, the sky darkening, until it was like night.

Was there? What other explanation was there?

But it was not night but the afternoon, and then the skies opened and rain fell in torrents, and all that evening, and still I sat on and on.

THE AUTHOR

James Ferron Anderson was born in Northern Ireland, where he worked as an egg packer, weaver, glassblower and soldier. He moved with his family to England, where he began to write in many forms, including poetry, short stories, plays and, more recently, novels. One of his first short stories, *The Bog Menagerie*, won the prestigious Bryan MacMahon Short Story Award in his native Ireland. He won the Escalator Award in his adopted England with *I Still Miss Someone*. He is a Writers' Centre Free Reads winner. *Something to Do*, another short story, was broadcast on Short Story Radio. *The River and The Sea* is his first novel.

He lives with his wife and two children in Norwich, and spends part of each year in British Columbia, Canada.

The River and The Sea was The Winner of the
Rethink Press New Novels 2012 Competition.

Rumour by Angela Lawrence won the
Best East Anglian Novel award.

Dead Letter Day by Keri Beevis was Runner Up.

For more information about Rethink Press and the
New Novels Competition visit www.rethinkpress.com

CPSIA information can be obtained at www.ICGtesting.com
Printed in the USA
LVOW121859070413

327998LV00003B/345/P